STRAY DOGS

Scott Braswell and Michael Braswell

Second Street Press

ISBN: 1535505605
ISBN 13: 9781535505604

ACKNOWLEDGMENTS

Some of these stories have previously appeared in a book published by Carolina Academic Press. We want to thank Editor Beth Hall for her help with that endeavor. The stories and characters depicted in this book are fictional. The authors also want to thank Susan Braswell for her help in getting this collection ready for publication.

CONTENTS

1

SARAH SALVATION

Like a cockroach seduced by a bug light, Francis Quiet Moon shuffled to the edge of an unmarked street corner and stared into the flickering pulse of a streetlamp. A frayed, mustard-yellow knit cap nearly swallowed his head and his tired frame ached from behind the stained, gas-station-attendant's shirt he was wearing. A tattered American flag was tied around his waist—some of the stars had been filled in by different colored crayons, courtesy of his two sons who lived with their mother. His feet were decorated by red and green bowling shoes two sizes too big.

With the remains of his existence stuffed into his Vietnam issue duffel bag, Francis had hitchhiked, but mostly walked his way through the last 100 miles of hill country, traveling the cracked back of a stubborn two-lane that twisted and curled around the Carolina mountains like a serpent. When he walked, the dog tags around his neck clinked like the teeth of a chattering skull. The sound made Francis uncomfortable and he thought about how something as insignificant as two pieces of metal hitting each other could bring back so many bad memories—before and after the war. At one time, Francis had built wind chimes in the cramped basement of the garage apartment he rented with his wife. He couldn't stand the sound of them anymore. They made his head hurt and his heart ache. At night, he would try to force those memories away, make them set with the sun. But every morning they would rise again, burning into his back as he walked, never letting him forget.

He had been losing his grip on sobriety since dawn and had to concentrate just to keep his balance. Francis cringed as the sounds of a honky-tonk version of Sinatra's "My Way" crackled from a nearby convenience store. Picking at the loose threads of his toboggan, he retrieved a near-empty bottle of "Cisco" brand liquor from beneath the remnants of Old Glory. He would often, as he described it, "Disco with Cisco," referring to the bottle as his faithful friend, "Fran-Cisco." The bottle spilled the truth to Francis in a numbing language he could understand. It never cheated on him, never lied to him, or blamed him for a failed marriage. It never confronted him with his past or promised him a future. Although "Fran-Cisco" had been his best friend since a rehab stint after the war, the relationship was stormy. But at least it was his. At least, he could depend on it.

He closed his eyes, took two quick, punishing gulps and gritted his teeth. Peeling open his left eye to squint, Francis could barely make out the lettering of a neon-crimson sign that spelled *Crystal Grape Diner*. Lured by the aroma of food, he slowly gathered up his road-weary carcass and stumbled across the intersection.

Francis stepped inside the diner and slid into a tattered, lime green booth patched by gray duct tape. Sounds from a Crosby, Stills, Nash & Young forty-five wafted from an elaborate jukebox squatting in a smoky corner of the diner like some kind of mechanized Sumo wrestler. Francis' hollow eyes scanned the surroundings for signs of activity while his fingers fumbled with a half-empty pack of Marlboro Lights. He thought about how he used to never smoke. His wife hated it.

Settling on a smoke that seemed dry enough to ignite, Francis lit up. Inhaling deeply, he ran his hands through his hair and observed the other examples of aimless humanity around him. An elderly man in a wheelchair, hooked up to an oxygen tank and dressed in a threadbare tuxedo, played solitaire at one booth. He would light a fresh cigarette every few minutes and let it burn on the edge of an ashtray; never smoking it, just letting it burn.

Francis' eyes followed a succession of Elvis paintings to the other side of the room where a small ruckus was erupting. He extinguished his cigarette on a small tin ashtray and peered through the smoke. A young woman, dressed in a checkered apron and combat boots, was juggling steak sauce bottles, three and four at a time to the cackling delight of four elderly, drunken La-Z-Boy warriors. After finishing her performance, the waitress took a modest bow, laid the party's check on the table and disappeared into the kitchen. The old men applauded her and were still snorting with laughter as they began to eat their food.

Francis was about to light up another Marlboro when he caught the scent of a pleasant fragrance. A smudged menu slid gently across his knuckles as he lit the cigarette and looked up. Smiling lips asked to take his order. Francis looked above the lips, into eyes warm and dark—shimmering as if fireflies were trapped inside. The tag artfully stitched onto her shirt said "Sarah." She glanced at his duffel bag while fumbling in her pocket for a pen.

"Where ya headed?" she inquired.

"Home," Francis replied in a raspy voice brought on by the late autumn cold.

"Where's home?"

"Don't know yet," he answered, grinning and rubbing his head.

She smiled to herself and nodded while pulling out her pad and pencil to take his order.

"What are your specials tonight?" Francis mumbled.

"Honey, everything I make is special."

Francis drew deeply from his cigarette and grinned so wide his face hurt.

"Well, how about a special cheeseburger and some special fries?"

The woman chuckled while taking down his order.

"You're pretty good with those bottles," he added, putting out another cigarette.

"Oh, yeah," she said, laughing. "Well, the way I see it, everybody has a special talent and I guess juggling Heinz 57 bottles for the enjoyment of my red-eyed regulars is mine."

"Aren't you afraid of dropping one of those bottles on someone's head or something?" Francis inquired, rubbing his chapped nose. "You know, with all the lawsuits these days, and what not?"

She smiled and took the menu from his trembling fingers.

"Sometimes you gotta do something risky to make sure you're still alive," she whispered. "Something special, coming up."

She smiled at Francis and clomped off in her combat boots toward the kitchen.

Francis laughed to himself and shook his head in amazement. Taking a last draw from his cigarette, he looked out the window and watched a couple of young boys in the shadows across the street, kicking an old cardboard box around. He wondered what their names were. His head began to hurt.

He wondered what his own boys were doing, what they had for dinner, what they dreamed about. Francis wondered if they wondered about him. Lighting another cigarette, he thought about how his boys used to always be in his dreams. These visions were like mirrors stitched on his heart, reflecting a time long since past. The last dream he had was like something out of a movie. It involved a big spread of blue sky that looked like a movie screen in the middle of a dark space. One arm, with the palm open, came in from one side of the sky and another arm, a boy's, came reaching across from the other side of the sky. Both arms were wrapped in barbed wire and reached for each other. That was all Francis could remember. He didn't know what it meant and hesitated to think about it too much, but it haunted him.

Francis finished his meal, laid a few wrinkled bills on the table, and hauled himself and his bag back out into the cold. A crushed velvet night covered him and he stared into its million eyes—"God's peepholes," as his grandmother once called them. The frigid night air filled his lungs and he turned toward the *Crystal Grape,* lighting another cigarette.

The half-lit neon sign whirred and popped, making the little shambled building stand out in the shadows like a kind of beacon. A faded "Help Wanted" sign rattled against a storm window.

"Sometimes you have to do something risky to make sure you're still alive." Sarah's words rolled around in what was left of Francis' pinball mind. He stood in the quiet moonlight and looked down the desolate stretch of road that brought him to this place. Putting out his cigarette, Francis turned his head and walked back inside.

2

SPECIAL OF THE WEEK

"It's cold as a witch's teat out there," Jimmy "Fastball" Burns exclaimed as he bustled through the main entrance of "Everybody Rides" used car lot, passing out cheeseburgers, fries and steaming cups of coffee.

"I ain't never seen a cold spell like this in the middle of December."

"You got that right!" Sam Jenkins, who was also known as Sam "Batboy" Jenkins, chimed in.

Buzz "Homerun" Renfro took a sip of coffee. "Why don't you two yahoos shut up and pass me some fries before they get cold."

J.J. "Coach" Moran, the Manager, looked at the three salesmen with mild disgust, the way a father would look at his rambunctious children. "Why don't all three of you quiet down so I can finish this here book on Joe DiMaggio, the greatest baseball player who ever lived."

"Everybody Rides" was actually the budget used car lot of the mega-dealership, "King of the Road Jaguar/Chrysler/Dodge/Kia." In automobile sales, this was the bottom of the barrel. The good used cars were on display in a paved lot adjoining the new car dealership. "Everybody Rides" was located two blocks from the other lots. "King of the Road" owner, Wild Bill Hancock, didn't want a car lot that proudly displayed in bright red letters under its name—NOTHING OVER $3995 and YOUR JOB IS YOUR CREDIT—to be too closely associated with the classier side of his business. As added punishment, "Everybody Rides" had to stay open until 10 p.m. each night while the rest of the dealership closed at 9:00 p.m.

If an outside observer were to come to the conclusion that Coach had a thing for baseball, he or she would be right on the money. He had coached Little League baseball for over thirty years and never had a winning season, but to hear him tell it, he had always been one hit or pitch away from baseball glory.

The only sounds in the office that evening were the sounds of four men inhaling their supper as they chewed, gulped and belched their way down to the last french fry. Each man had his own story of what brought him to this place. Coach had successfully managed the upscale used car lot for ten years before he punched out an opposing Little League coach who happened to be the cousin of Wild Bill Hancock. The others were exiled to "Everybody Rides" for different reasons and in keeping with his passion for baseball, Coach had given each of his "players" a nickname.

Jimmy "Fastball" Burns had been the leading Dodge truck salesman for three years in a row. Nobody knew more about pick-up trucks than he did and nobody could close a truck sale as quickly as he could. Unfortunately, "Fastball" decided to celebrate his third divorce by driving off in a brand new loaded Dodge Club Cab that he hadn't cleared with the manager. With a fifth of Jim Beam riding shotgun, he totaled the truck and his sales career.

Sam "Batboy" Jenkins was a wiry fellow with nervous eyes. Coach had named him "Batboy" because as he frequently reminded him: "Boy, you ain't even in the game. You can't score, if you don't get to the plate." Coach used to call Sam "Third String" Jenkins, but after three consecutive months at the bottom of the sales ladder, demoted him to "Batboy."

Sam was the only one of the four men who had never been married. In fact, he had allegedly only had two dates and one didn't count—the occasion of his senior prom when he paid his next-door neighbor, Debbie Ann Muskgrove twenty dollars to accompany him. Rumor had it that he offered to pay her another five dollars for a goodnight kiss.

The truth was that Debbie Ann told Sam that the only part of her he could kiss for five dollars was her ass.

Coach was married to his second wife; "Fast ball" was, as he liked to put it, currently "playing the field;" and Buzz also divorced, was heavily involved with Darlene, a former dancer with "Sand and Sun Cruise Lines." She was presently employed as senior nail technician for "The New You Salon."

Buzz and Darlene had been going together for more than a year and although he had told no one, he was planning to pop the question on New Year's Eve.

Leaning back in an office chair with his feet propped up on his desk, Buzz fingered the gold-plated money clip in his left front pocket that secured the five one hundred dollar bills he had saved to buy Darlene's engagement ring. He smiled in anticipation of her excitement. No one could get as excited as Darlene. Buzz's daydream was abruptly interrupted by the grating voice of Jimmy "Fastball" Burns.

"Customer on the lot. It's your turn Renfro," he bellowed.

Buzz lit a Camel and peered out the office window into the cold, black December night. Who would be looking for a used car at 8:45 on a cold Saturday night? Blowing a spiral of smoke rings toward the ceiling, Buzz said, "Why don't we give them a few minutes to see if they are really serious."

Without taking his eyes off the page he was reading, Coach took charge of the situation: "Batter up Renfro. Get your ass out there and into scoring position. Batboy, you're in the on deck circle."

Batboy grinned at Buzz. "I done taken a peek Homerun. I can tell from here, she ain't much to look at and more'n likely she ain't got no money. Them two kids means she ain't got no man which means she ain't got no money which means you ain't gonna make no money. Comprendez, Amigo?"

Buzz blew another series of smoke rings toward the door. "Two things, Batboy: First, I'm not your Amigo and second, can you comprendez that?"

Zipping up his parka, Buzz ground out the remnants of his cigarette in the ashtray, closed the door behind him and stepped out into the cold night.

Agnes was cold and not just from the threadbare parka she was wearing, but cold deep inside, down in her bones. She felt like her heart was almost frozen shut—like it was barely beating. The only thing on this freezing December night that gave her any warmth was her son, Kenny, and her daughter, Sonja. And they gave her just enough to keep her going a while longer. Ten years seemed like a lifetime ago when she up and married their father, a truck driver twenty years her senior. They met at the small mountain top café where she had worked as a waitress. Harold had promised her the good life, but what he had given her was too many years of misery. He finally left her and the children two years ago with unpaid bills and no goodbyes.

Agnes wasn't a woman given to bitterness, she was just tired. Somehow, having Kenny and Sonja made the misery worth the trouble. At eight and six, they were still young enough to make up the difference between the poverty and hopelessness with a few well-practiced dreams, the most recent incarnation being what Santa Claus might bring them. At least it seemed to be so as far as Sonja was concerned. Agnes wasn't as sure about Kenny. He acted happy enough, but she had seen the sad, uncertain look in his eyes when he thought she wasn't paying attention.

Working two jobs, one at a nursing home and the other at Taco Bell didn't make for much of a life. They had been evicted from their apartment for unpaid rent three days after her truck had been repossessed. Agnes had no illusions about her chances of getting the salesman walking towards her to sell her a car for a fifty-dollar down payment, but fifty dollars was all she had.

"How do you do, Ma'am? You got a couple of fine looking children. Name's Buzz Renfro. What can I do for you?"

Agnes looked at the salesman for several moments before she spoke. "Mr. Renfro, my name's Agnes Davis and these here are my children, Kenny and Sonja. We are in great need of a reliable vehicle."

"Yes ma'am. Well, you've come to the right place because "reliable" is our middle name. Every vehicle we sell has undergone a 21 point inspection."

"Mama," Sonja interrupted, " I'm hungry!"

"Hush Sonja, we'll get something to eat when we finish our business with Mr. Renfro."

Dropping her head at the tone of reprimand in Agnes's voice, Sonja buried her face in Kenny's jacket.

"Tell you what kids, how 'bout candy bars and cokes on me while your mother and I check out the cars," Buzz offered, pulling four one dollar bills out of his pocket.

"I couldn't let you do that, Mr. Renfro," Agnes protested.

"I ain't hungry anyway," Kenny added, stuffing his hands in the pockets of his denim jacket.

"Well, I am," Sonja exclaimed, peering from behind the folds of her brother's jacket.

"Hey, I insist," Buzz responded. "Besides, you'll be warm inside. Ask for a Mr. Moran when you get inside. He'll show you where the goodies are."

Agnes relented and Kenny took the three dollars and Sonja by the hand and proceeded toward the office. Buzz lit another cigarette as he and Agnes stood watching the vapor trail of Kenny and Sonja's breathing as they made their way toward food and warmth.

"Now, Mrs. Davis, what would you like to look at? We only have about an hour until we close."

Agnes' eyes escorted her children into the office. "Mr. Renfro, I'm going to be honest with you. I'm in desperate need of a vehicle. I have two children, two jobs—if I can come up with transportation—nowhere to live, and fifty dollars in my right coat pocket."

Buzz took a deep draw from his cigarette before he spoke.

"Ma'am, please don't take this the wrong way, but sounds to me like you need a lot more help than just a vehicle—at least more help than I can give you. You need to get a hold of some area churches or the Human Services Department or something else like that. Besides, the cheapest vehicle on our lot requires a down payment of several hundred dollars. Maybe you ought to call your family."

Agnes turned her head slightly to compose herself. "No offense taken, Mr. Renfro. Don't have no family, but I'll figure something out."

She took a deep breath and extended her hand. "I want to thank you for the kindness you showed my children. I'll be fetchin' them now."

"Well, Ma'am, at least let me get you a hot cup of coffee."

"Thank you, but that won't be necessary," Agnes replied as she walked toward the office, leaving Buzz to ponder the crisp night air.

"Hellfire," Buzz muttered to himself. "Why do I always have to get the hard-luck customers? Life's tough for *everybody*."

He could see Kenny's and Sonja's faces peering out of the office window as their mother approached them and thought to himself, Where will they go? What'll happen to them? What does it matter to me? It don't.

All Buzz had on his mind was the wad of cash in his pocket and Darlene. He popped a piece of chewing gum in his mouth and pretended to check the cars on the lot. He also pretended it would be less embarrassing for Agnes and her kids if he waited until they left.

Buzz watched as Agnes and her children made their way across the car lot toward the bus stop on the corner.

As they started to cross the street, Sonja turned and waved to him and shouted, "Hey Mister! Thank you for the candy. I hope you have a Merry Christmas!"

It was at that precise moment that Buzz Renfro went temporarily insane.

He might as well have been hit by a meteor from outer space. The gold plated money clip in his pant's pocket seemed to turn white hot. He felt dizzy, his knees buckled slightly, and even with the chill of the night air, Buzz could feel a bead of sweat break out on his forehead.

Somewhere between Sonja's "Merry" and "Christmas," something—some great mystery—traveling faster than the speed of light, had penetrated Buzz Renfro and knocked him senseless. In that moment, the fake gold nugget ring on his right hand ceased to exist. Even the image of Darlene became little more than a dancing shadow. Buzz was pulled out of himself into a place he had never been before. It was as if he was having an out of body experience, observing himself running toward Agnes and her two children who were standing under the street light, waiting on the rest of their lives.

As he ran, his mind was saying stop, but his legs weren't listening.

When he caught up with them, Buzz bent over and grabbed his knees, breathing heavily.

"Mr. Renfro, are you all right?" Buzz took a deep breath, sucking the cold air into his lungs. "Yes ma'am, I believe I am. It just occurred to me that we might have a vehicle suitable to your needs."

"But I told you, I only have. . . ."

Buzz interrupted her, "I forgot to tell you about the special of the week. If you could use a 1992 minivan, you could drive it away tonight for no down payment and one hundred and twenty-five dollars a month."

"I don't know what to say," Agnes' eyes widened.

"Say yes, Mama. Say yes!" Sonja exclaimed, jumping up and down as Kenny looked on silently.

"Yes," Agnes said, her face freed up the hint of a smile, the first she had felt in weeks.

Agnes with her coffee and Kenny and Sonja with their hot chocolate waited in the customer lounge while Buzz filled out the paper work.

Batboy shook his head. "I would've bet a month's pay that lady wouldn't have two cents to her name. Can't believe she's got the cash for the down payment."

"Well believe it," Buzz replied as he signed the last of the finance forms.

Draining the last of his coffee, Coach looked solemnly at Buzz and cleared his throat, "Well, Homerun, it wasn't one of our better units—certainly not of home-run caliber, but I will give you an infield hit."

Buzz handed Agnes the keys. Even Kenny seemed excited. Not like Sonja, but at least pleased. Looking at the keys in her hand, Agnes didn't say anything. Instead, she put her arms around Buzz and placed her head on his chest. He didn't know what else to do so he hugged her.

As the minivan left the lot of "Everybody Rides," all Buzz could see was the smiling face of Sonja pressed against the rear glass window. Her smile went right through him. His fingers grazed the empty money clip. It wasn't hot any more. And he knew Darlene probably wouldn't be coming down his chimney on Christmas Eve. Opening a fresh pack of cigarettes, Buzz looked up at the glittering stars and said to no one in particular, "Merry 'hotdamn' Christmas."

3

THE OPEN DOOR

Just about everyone called my Grandfather "Pappa Jim", although I'm not sure why. Pappa Jim and his father were both born and raised in the sleepy farming community of Ashton. My mother, who was his and Grandmama's middle child, said it was because he was kind and helpful to everyone, which was for the most part true. He was always giving away garden vegetables to neighbors and strangers alike. When a barn burned, Pappa Jim would be the first one to show up with his toolbox in hand—even if the barn happened to belong to old man Stringfellow. Stringfellow (or "String-along", as he was known by the locals) once sold a tractor he had promised Pappa Jim to someone else because the man in question had offered him five dollars more. I remember asking Pappa Jim one time why he would help somebody who had treated him and countless others so badly.

Amused, he sized up my ten-year-old indignation and chuckled.

"Stringfellow's kind needs our help the most. Maybe if he gets enough help with whatever's been sticking in his craw all these years, he'll come to realize that there's more satisfaction in helping somebody than taking advantage of them."

I can't say a young boy's logic agreed with the wisdom of my Grandfather, but that was the way he was. Pappa Jim didn't hold grudges. He forgave others their faults as easily as he seemed to forget his own shortcomings.

One afternoon, when I asked my Dad why he thought everyone referred to my grandfather as Pappa Jim, he thought for several minutes before responding. Lighting his pipe and exhaling a lazy curl of smoke, he concluded it must be because of Pappa Jim's sense of humor, and that he was a natural storyteller. He had a joke or funny anecdote for every occasion and often brought a smile to even the dourest acquaintance. When Pappa Jim told a story people seemed to laugh in spite of themselves.

I asked Grandmama the same question. She looked at me, threw her head back and laughed.

"Child, you are something. Now go get yourself one of those sugar cookies while I pour you a glass of milk."

It was always like that. Food was the currency of Grandmama's conversations and her response to most queries.

I never did figure out why everyone called my Grandfather Pappa Jim. I came to believe it was because he looked and acted like the Grandfather everyone secretly wished they had. Although everyone called me Jamie, my real name was Jim, just like his. I was proud to be named after him. He was my best friend. It's true enough we had our disagreements from time to time, but like best friends usually do, we made up in short order. Pappa Jim taught me to work and play. The hot, tedious labor of farming and gardening was rewarded in the season of ripening and harvest. He also taught me how to whittle, hunt quail and rabbits, and most importantly, fish. Nobody loved fishing more than Pappa Jim and me, and there was no place we enjoyed that vocation more than at the lake on Pappa Jim's farm. He even built a special bench near the dam where we could sit under the shade of a towering oak, which he called "Old Bertha." We would sit under that tree and while away the long hot summer, talking and laughing, and eating the sandwiches Grandmama had prepared for us. On occasion, we would catch a mess of fish, which would end up as the main course for the evening's meal. I still remember the first fish I caught—a small crappie. I was only five and couldn't believe my good fortune at catching six fish in quick succession. It wasn't until years later that I found out why I had been such a successful angler. Pappa Jim would distract my attention by showing me the ducks or some other sight while he threw the hooked crappie back into the water for me to reel in once again. I have always felt sorry for that fish. But to a five year old, it was magic.

In a way, Pappa Jim was a Grandfather to everybody in Ashton. If they needed guidance or advice, he was there for them. Of course, Grandmama didn't call him Pappa Jim. She called him Jimmy, which never sounded right to me. And his three life-long friends, Vernon, Max, and Clarence, with whom he hunted, fished, and on the first and second Friday of each month, played poker, didn't call him Pappa Jim. Vernon called him Jimbo, Max called him Big Jim and Clarence referred to him as "J." I always found it interesting that he and I were both named Jim, yet nobody called us by our real names.

I guess you could say Pappa Jim was as close to perfect as Grandfathers go. As far as I could tell, he only had one real peccadillo that stood out: he would not let anyone open a door for him nor would he open the door for anyone else. His peccadillo even extended to my Grandmama. His daughters, including my Mother, used to occasionally chide him regarding his peculiar habit. But as always, Grandmama simply laughed and offered everyone a piece of cake, pie, or whatever other edible she had handy. When questioned about his conduct, Pappa Jim would typically respond with a shrug of his shoulders or a grunt of indifference. When confronted by his youngest daughter, Aunt Sue, on the occasion of entering the front door of the First Methodist Church for his and Grandmama's fiftieth wedding anniversary, he uncharacteristically bellowed, "Why don't you mind your own damned business?"

After that, no one, not even Aunt Sue, ever mentioned it again.

In June of 1991, I had my fourteenth birthday. In July, Pappa Jim turned 78. The week following his birthday found us sitting under the cool shade of Old Bertha, sipping Grandmama's sweet tea and fishing for catfish. Following her bout with cancer, Grandmama didn't cook as much as she used to, but she still had plenty of sugar cookies, cakes and pies, compliments of the local Piggly Wiggly.

It was one of those hot, humid, hazy summer afternoons. Pappa Jim and me weren't sure whether we wanted to fish or take a nap under Old Bertha's protective shade. When he finished the last of his tea, Pappa Jim wiped his khaki shirtsleeve across his mouth.

"Jamie, you're fourteen. Caught between childhood and manhood. You got any questions your old Pappa Jim might need to give an answer to? Like the birds and the bees? You know those girly magazines like the one your old Grandmama found under your mattress last Saturday morning don't necessarily give you the real low down."

I said nothing and looked down at my feet, gingerly holding my reel and rod. I didn't have to say anything. My beet-red face said it all.

Suddenly, Pappa Jim roared with laughter and slapped his right knee.

"Boy, don't worry about it. It's natural to be curious at your age. You know where to find me if you want to talk about it."

Pappa Jim leaned back against the trunk of the old oak tree and pulled the bill of his fishing cap down over his eyes.

"Pappa Jim, I do have one question."

I hesitated to proceed.

After a few moments, Pappa Jim raised the bill of his cap and looked at me. "Well Jamie, what is it? What's on your mind?"

"Why don't you let people open doors for you and why don't you open the door for Grandmama?"

Still reclining against Old Bertha, Pappa Jim looked at me for a long time before responding. When he did finally did, he had a far away look in his eyes, a look that made me wish I could take the question back. It was as though he was looking at something in the distance that I couldn't see.

"Jamie, meet me at the house day after tomorrow after you get home from school. I'm going to show you something. You're fourteen now. Maybe it'll do you some good. Only thing I ask is that you not tell anyone else until after I'm gone."

Wide-eyed at the prospect of our shared secret, I quickly agreed. I slept little that night, trying to imagine what the secret might be.

At the appointed time, I bounded up the steps to my Grandparent's house.

"Pappa Jim," I shouted.

Grandmama spoke from the kitchen, "Jimmy's waiting for you in his truck."

We rode in silence for a few miles before we turned into an old, ill-kept graveyard on the edge of town.

I followed Pappa Jim's quick pace to the back left corner of the cemetery. He stopped in front of three small gravestones, kneeled down and began pulling up the few weeds that had sprung up around the well-kept area. When he finished, he spread a small bouquet of fresh cut flowers in front of the three headstones. The names were barely legible.

"You know who these three fellows were?" Pappa Jim asked, rising to his feet and dusting off his pants.

"I can barely read their names Pappa Jim."

"Their names are Ben Smith, Eli Johnson and Johnny Smith."

"Ring any bells?" Pappa Jim continued, looking quietly at the headstones.

"No, Sir."

"They were the three black boys who were hung by a mob in the fall of 1933 for raping a young white girl." Pappa Jim turned and looked at me, his eyes soft and somber. "They were hung by a mob for doin' something they never did. The girl's boyfriend cooked up the whole story and she went along with it. That story ended up getting three innocent boys killed. Course, nobody around these parts likes to talk much about what happened."

"That's a really terrible thing, but what has it got to do with you?"

Continuing to look at me with a sadness I had never seen in him before, Pappa Jim fished an old, faded newspaper clipping out of his shirt pocket and handed it to me. I took it from him and read it carefully. The title of the article declared in bold print: "Three Negro Rapists Receive Their Just Rewards!"

"Like I said before, Pappa Jim, it was a terrible thing, but I still don't see what it has to do with you?"

"Look closely at the photograph Jamie. What do you see?"

I studied the faded picture as closely as I could.

"I see a mob pushing three young black men out of the jail into the street."

"See the young man holding the jail door open?"

"Yessir."

Pappa Jim sighed, "That young man is me."

Not knowing what else to do, I handed the faded clipping back to him. He carefully folded it before returning it to his pocket. We stood in silence for a long time.

"Pappa Jim, I know you feel bad about what happened, but that was a long time ago. You were barely a man. And besides, you didn't hang those boys; you just held the door open."

Pappa Jim looked at me, his eyes flashing with pain and anger.

"I was a damn fool and more importantly, I was old enough to know better."

"But Pappa Jim, you didn't hang anybody!"

"No Jamie, I didn't hang anybody, I just held the door open for the ones who did. I opened a door that I should've closed."

"But Pappa Jim. . . . "

"No buts about it, I was a part of that heartless, murdering mob. I came to my senses when I saw them stringing those boys up in the town square. But even then, I remained silent. Those three boys, Ben, Eli and Johnny were only 15 or 16 years old. They had Mamas and Papas and dreams, just like me and you. "

Pappa Jim's voice began to crack as his eyes filled with tears. I had never seen my Grandfather cry.

"There ain't a day goes by that I haven't thought about those three boys and my part in their death. Ben proclaimed his innocence once or twice and then became silent as they placed the noose around his neck. But you could see the anger and hurt in his eyes as he looked out on that hate-filled crowd for the last time. Eli just closed his eyes and sang some kind of spiritual song until the life was choked out of him. Poor Johnny was the youngest and the most pitiful. He messed on himself and called for his Mama while the crowd laughed at him. After it was over, I cried all the way home and I've cried many a tear since. But the truth is, I was a part of that 'terrible thing' as you call it."

My Mama was so disappointed when she saw my picture in the paper that she didn't speak to me for a long time. She and I both knew she had raised me better than that. Fact is the only honorable man in Ashton on that dark day was Arthur Johannsen. He ran a local funeral parlor and was the only person who would take the bodies. During that time, this cemetery was for whites only, but Johannsen bought the plots himself and gave the three boys a proper burial, even though it upset some of the locals. To this day, it's understood by all the black folks in Ashton that when one of them dies, they take their business to Johannsen Funeral Home.

"I come up here every year on the anniversary of the lynching and talk to Ben, Eli and Johnny."

With that said, Pappa Jim dropped to one knee and bowed his head. Standing next to him, I bowed my head as well.

After several minutes of silence, Pappa Jim rose to his feet and walked slowly to his truck.

We rode back to the farm, neither of us speaking a word. When we pulled up to the farmhouse, Pappa Jim turned off the ignition. He turned to me with a sad smile and patted me on the knee.

"So you see, Jamie, your Pappa Jim's not the man you thought he was."

From somewhere deep within, I felt the tears rising inside me. Wiping my eyes, I looked at my Grandfather, not sure what to say.

"Everyone makes mistakes."

"That's right, Jamie. But if I'm going to be real to you, you got to know me for who I am—warts and all. Lord knows I have my faults, chief among them the terrible suffering Ben, Eli and Johnny went through that I played a part in. For our bond to be strong, you and me have to be straight with each other. It's important that you learn something from my mistakes. Maybe some small good can come from the bad that I've been a part of. I know I've put a lot on you this afternoon. I'd be lying if I didn't tell you that in a way, it feels good to let you in on my secret—to maybe let you help me carry my burden in some small way. If this afternoon means anything, I need to know what you've learned from what I've told and shown you."

Pappa Jim waited patiently while I pondered what he said.

"I guess I learned a couple of things," I answered. "What appears to be ain't necessarily so. Nobody's perfect, even the ones you love. And if you love someone, you love them even if they've done something bad. Sometimes we have to carry the bad 'cause we can't make it right. We still have to try—to do the best we can even when it doesn't feel like enough."

I took a deep breath and looked into Pappa Jim's eyes. He said nothing, but his eyes were full of love and compassion. They looked like they were a thousand years old.

Now I'm thirty-four, married with a wife and two children. It's been twenty years since that afternoon and ten years since Pappa Jim passed on, but I often think about our days together.

Last night I dreamed I was fishing under the shade of Old Bertha with four elderly black men. They were talking mostly among themselves. As I rose to leave, one of them turned to me with a twinkle in his eye and said, "Jamie, have you caught any crappie lately?"

4

THUNDER FOR MALLY

S till clouds stitched a sky that burned a deep Chevy blue as Moses McCready plowed his 18-wheeled monster toward Lavonia. Moses believed that every road had its own distinct personality and old Bloody 98, which split the state of Georgia right down the middle, was especially sinister. Its cracked face was haunted by the ghosts of burning tire tread and pockmarked by dips and gulleys that could scare the warranty off of the most expensive radials.

A radio wire was wrapped around Moses' leg like a blacksnake dipped in Jeri Curl, and he licked his lips in eager anticipation of the on-air antics of Prime Minister 66— the reclusive self-proclaimed "Apostle of the Airwaves" who hosted a closed-circuit radio talk show for truckers called "Finger Lickin' Good."

Moses had once wanted the words "pride" and "prejudice" tattooed on each of his shoulders. Though inspired by Robert Mitchum's character in *Night of the Hunter* who had the words "Love" and "Hate" inscribed on his knuckles, Moses preferred a place less seen by public eyes. He was never one to draw a lot of attention to himself. His shoulders—which his ex-wife once admiringly referred to as "the scales of justice"—seemed perfectly appropriate for grand abstractions.

Unfortunately, on a hot August night, an intoxicated Moses wandered into a Valdosta tattoo parlor and commenced to insult the multiple piercings of the owner and resident artist. Angered and blessed with the foresight to recognize a potentially diabolical opportunity, the artist inscribed Moses' shoulders with the words "prude" and "prejudiced," instead of "pride" and "prejudice." This act of skin art sabotage caused Moses much embarrassment and resulted in his subsequent resignation from the esteemed Southeastern American Trucker's Association—The Wayward Rollers of Waskee-Gee.

Moses reached for his radio dial to turn up the volume and laughed at the Prime Minister's throaty musings when he realized that Marna Van's café would be rolling into view in a matter of moments. Choosing between the Prime Minister's verbal hailstorms and Marna's homemade banana pudding was always a struggle for Moses but *tonight,* Sissy Van's truck was at the café.

And Moses liked Sissy.

When he noticed her poorly parked vehicle gracing the grounds he nearly flipped his truck in an effort to careen into the parking lot. Sissy Van had the kind of slingshot smile that could blow your kneecaps out.

After hesitating at the door to adjust himself, Moses walked inside the café and took his hat off. Petulia Jackson occupied her usual corner—sucking down Cherry Cokes and cutting celebrity faces out of magazines. As Moses walked by, Petulia's black eyes seemed to get smaller and more round, like the barrels of a twenty-two. She never had to say anything to him. A look like that was enough.

Sissy appeared from behind the counter and unveiled one of those smiles. "You goin' racin' this weekend?" she asked.

"Yeah, tomorrow night," Moses replied, tracing his finger around the brim of his hat. "Got Ginger's ride in the truck."

Sissy looked puzzled. "Ginger Pervis?"

"Do you know another *man* named Ginger?"

A thin smile crawled across Sissy's face. "Awright smarty. I didn't know he was out of prison."

"For the last month or so," Moses replied, lighting a Camel cigarette. "We'll see if he can keep it that way."

"You don't sound so sure."

"Well, sometimes the past ain't somethin' you just shake off your pant leg."

"We all make mistakes, Moses," she said, nodding at him and arching an eyebrow.

Moses put his hat back on and clasped his hands together. "Some of us make 'em. Others make an industry out of 'em."

Sissy shook her head and wiped her mouth with her wrist.

"This is for you," she said, putting a lid on a styrofoam cup packed with pudding. Moses averted his eyes as she licked her fingers.

She wiped the excess pudding off another cup and handed the cup to him.

"And give this to your brother. Tell him not to be a stranger."

"Ginger don't like banana puddin'," Moses grunted.

"Well, then, I'm sure you can find some use for it," she said, smiling and patting his stomach. "What are you, about a forty-six now?"

"I'm a solid forty-two, honey."

"No, I didn't ask you your age, Moses. I was talking about your waist."

Moses chuckled and walked toward the door. "Why can't you be as funny as you are pretty? It's a rule, you know. The good-lookin' ones just don't have a sense of humor."

"Goodnight, funnyman," Sissy chuckled as he closed the door.

Rain started to fall as Moses lumbered toward his truck, thinking about Sissy's pudding-spattered fingers.

He gently rested one hand on his bulging stomach, tapping his own digits. Slipping another cigarette between his lips, he pulled his hat tightly over his head and looked up into the bruised black sky.

"Damn rain."

The waving arms of trees painted stripes like cell bars across Mally DeVaney's face as she looked out the window and watched the sun slide down the sky. She was a thin-boned child, with a small frame and large brown eyes that some people found unnerving. This was her favorite time of the day, and the evening had always brought comfort. She remembered the times her mother would hold her in a rocking chair on the front porch and sing her favorite hymns. But she was too old for all of that now. Eleven-year-olds don't sit in laps—especially eleven-year-old paraplegic girls who, from an early age have felt the sting of staring eyes and poisoned words.

Built by her grandfather, Mally's wheelchair was designed as a replica of the "El Diablo," the demolition derby classic driven by her all-time favorite demolition derby driver—Ginger "Pink Eye" Pervis.

Flaming hearts and whiskey breath are what Mally remembered when she thought about her father telling stories late into the night about eye-witness accounts of Ginger Pervis' driving prowess and the unholy sounds that bellowed from beneath the hood of the "El Diablo."

Mally's father said the car's engine was so loud it would shake his belt buckle loose. She remembered listening to gasoline and whiskey-soaked tales and staring at her father's shoulder, tracing the flaming heart tattoo with her finger, over and over until she drifted off to sleep.

Deep in the night Mally used to awake to the sounds of her father serenading her from a tangle of tree limbs. After walking home from the late shift, he would often climb the big Weeping Willow near her bedroom window and softly sing to her until she fell back asleep. Sometimes he would blow smoke rings at her and she would count and see how long it took for them to shatter against the windowsill.

The tree leaves whispered outside the window as Mally thought back to the first time her father took her to a race. She remembered nervously wrapping the frayed hem of her dress around a rusty nail that sprouted crookedly from the cracked wood bleacher. She remembered the crowd's drunken chorus as the hoarse gargle of engines wailed and grunted, grinding metal into metal and kicking up clouds of dust. Mally would rest her head against her father's chest and feel the pulse of his heart quicken with every firecracker piston pop.

Mally carefully packed away those memories in a special place as she watched the tree's crooked arms wave at her, and she imagined her father's spirit soaking their roots. Mel DeVaney, standing in the kitchen with a pile of hair stacked on her head, and a cigarette sprouting from between her fingers, watched her daughter at the window—her tiny lips muttering something to herself, breaths of wind gently lifting and lowering her long hair.

Mel rubbed the back of her neck and put out her cigarette. "Miss M., these dirty dishes are calling your name."

"Momma, can we go to the race tonight?" Mally asked, still staring out the window.

Mel smiled and shook her head. "Honey, I know this is my only night off—*our* night—but wouldn't you rather go to the show, or the lake, or somethin'?"

Mally rubbed her nose and turned her chair toward her mother. A few of daylight's drying rays spilled across her lap and onto the floor. The look in her eyes was the answer.

Mel sighed and bit her lower lip. "Let me guess. The El Diablo is in town." A smile hopscotched across Mally's narrow face. "Awright. I guess that means we're all catching 'pink eye' tonight, huh?"

"Oh, yeah!" Mally answered, wheeling herself into the kitchen.

They were all gonna be at the "Southlake Starlight Rally By The River" tonight.

Wiley Wiggins, a notorious driver/meat shop owner from Winston-Salem was expected to arrive in grand fashion. He would customarily tie meat-strung coat hangers onto his bumper before entering the stadium in hopes of attracting stray dogs. He always thought this made for a more grandiose entrance, although he often failed to attract even an occasional mongrel. The way Wiley saw it though—even if it didn't work it couldn't help but fatten his legend. He also had a skull with bat wings mounted on his hood and he wore a cowboy hat down over his eyes— eyes that few had ever seen. The brow of his hat curled down like a dead crow's talon and a string of bones would rattle when he walked. He had the words, "Oh, Shit!" painted on his hood in bright red letters. When asked why, Wiggins' reply was always the same: "Because that's what they say when they see me comin'."

Another character stuck in the thick of lore and infamy, The Grey Ghost, was apparently lured out of retirement just for this event. The Ghost wore white face paint and was given his title because no one ever saw him leave or arrive. For thirty-two years no one had ever heard him speak, either. But that had ended in Wilkesboro, NC when, then minutes before a race, the Ghost got locked in a Port-O-Potty. To make matters worse, someone had thrown in a rattlesnake just to make the situation a little more interesting. The perpetrator was never caught.

One of the crowd's favorites was T. "Hoppy" Hallahan, who had to move around each dirt track on a skateboard with a small lawnmower engine strapped on the tail.

According to rumor, his wife ran over him with his own car when she found out he had been sleeping around on her. Hallahan claims he was mobbed in an alleyway. But considering that his hometown of Hartland has a population of two-hundred thirty-eight, most joke that there aren't enough people there to form an opinion, much less a shin-breaking mob. Besides, accounts of Elka Hallahan and her jealous rages are of legend and almost always find their way into midnight story-telling sessions or early morning bar confessions.

And then there was Ginger "Pink Eye" Pervis.

Ginger had spent the last six years of his life in the Georgia State Penitentiary, where the only racing he did was from his bed to the toilet. In prison, Ginger was nicknamed "Squirt Gun" because of his frequent bouts with dysentery. He had spent much of his youth in and out of juvenile detention centers for various acts of teenage terrorism. At fourteen he had been arrested for his impressive collection of basketball rims, which had reportedly been taken from over thirty driveways and playgrounds around the county, including two taken from the high school gymnasium on the eve of the regional championship. Ginger's father died when he was young and his mother suffered from emotional problems. It was hard enough for her to deal with her own situation much less monitor the hormone-warped antics of a juvenile delinquent. One day, on the eve of his twenty-third birthday, Ginger—wild eyed and juiced up on a bottle of Fighting Cock brand liquor— hijacked a neighborhood ice cream truck in the middle of the day and drove it into the Powell River. On the way to the truck's watery grave, Ginger also managed to swerve and hit the Chief of Police's prize-winning seventeen-year-old Pomeranian show-dog. The truck got Ginger two years in prison. The dog got him four.

Though he secretly envied Ginger's rambunctious spirit, Moses resented his younger brother's lack of respect for their mother. Moses didn't even go to the trial.

With the exception of the dysentery and the development of a serious smoking habit, prison was good for Ginger. The silence was his therapist, advisor and advocate for change, forcing him to think about the wreck his life had become and about his mother whose memory haunted him. Ginger cried once in prison. And while some prisoners would often mock another inmate's expression of grief, dismissing him as fearful or weak, Ginger's crying carried a different tone—one of genuine pain and sorrow—and was met with only silence and sounds of its own echoes. Sometimes at night the moon would cast shadows on the ceiling of his room. They looked like continents crawling across the concrete and Ginger would try to identify them before they slipped away.

"Mac," Ginger Pervis yelled, pulling at a corner of his mustache, "I hate banana pudding, man. You know that."

"You're awful picky for a man who just got out of prison," Moses McCready snapped back, reaching into an old rusted orange toolbox. "Besides, if you knew who made it, you'd probably want seconds."

"Where'd you get it?"

"Marna's."

Ginger carefully sealed the lid back on the cup. "Sissy workin'?"

Moses nodded and disappeared beneath the hood of the El Diablo. Ginger's eyes glazed over and his mind sorted through old memories of a simpler time, time he was finding more and more difficult to remember. Pudding slid down the cup and dripped onto the floor.

"Hey, Mr. Pervis."

Ginger stared at the oil spots on the floor, lost.

"Ginger."

"What?" he mumbled, shaking his head and readjusting his eyes.

His eyes blurred and he blinked again. A girl, small and still, was sitting in one of the strangest looking wheelchairs Ginger had ever seen.

He took one look into the girl's eyes and they swallowed him.

Ginger twisted the same corner of his mustache. "I like your wheelchair," he said, hoping that didn't come out the wrong way.

"Thanks. It's the El Diablo. Well, not really. But kind of. My grandfather's version of it, anyway."

Ginger smiled and winced as he crouched down on his knees next to Mally. "You wanna see a Blackbird fly?" he asked to her obvious confusion.

"O.K."

"Alright, watch my eyebrows," Ginger directed, leaning in close to her face.

Ginger could move his eyes in a way that made his eyebrows move like flapping bird's wings. He once used this "gift" to charm the girls when he was a boy. These days the technique didn't exactly hold the same allure for the ladies. Of course, neither did being an ex-convict.

"Wow!" Mally gasped. "How come they do that!?"

"Hey, it's a talent, you know. Maybe I'm part bird or something," he said, trailing off and laughing softly.

"Sometimes I dream of flying like a bird," Mally said, nervously rubbing her nose—a habit her mother discouraged but couldn't stop. "Only I don't look like a bird in my dreams, except for big silver wings. Like on the hood of a Cadillac."

"I don't dream too much," Ginger said. "I wish I did though. You like Cadillacs?"

"They're O.K. Not loud enough."

"You like loud, huh?"

"My daddy used to take me to watch you drive. He said that one time you were so loud that you knocked this off," Mally said, pointing to an elaborate, chipped belt buckle she was wearing. A buckle that had the words *Takin' Care Of Business* on it.

"That's a mighty fine lookin' buckle you got there."

The piece looked outrageously large for her frail little body. Mally gripped her wheels with her little pale hands and turned toward the garage's exit. "Do you think you could do it again?" she asked, slowly wheeling away.

"Do what, honey?" Ginger said, pulling at his mustache.

"Make it *that* loud, again."

"How loud do you want it?" he whispered hoarsely as she rolled away.

"Like thunder," Mally answered. "Like God havin' a birthday party."

The little girl wheeled herself out of the garage. Ginger smiled and dropped his head, mouthing to himself the last few words Mally said to him. His gaze returned to the oil spots on the floor. They looked like continents.

"Mac," he called, twisting the corner of his mustache.

"Yeah."

"I need you to do something for me."

"I don't need to do anything. It's you who needs to do the doin'."

"What?"

"Quit pullin' on your mustache. It annoys the hell out of me."

"Oh, I'm sure it's not the only thing that annoys you ole boy."

"No, but it's way up on the list."

"Speaking of lists, you might want to cut some things off that grocery list," Ginger said, eyeing Moses' stomach suspiciously. "I'm gonna have to give your belly its own area code."

Moses' eyes twitched and the loose flesh on his soiled fingers constricted the heavy handle of a lug wrench. "You know, one time—a long, long time ago—when you were a little boy, I had a glimmer of hope for you. I bet the moment lasted twenty seconds, but it was twenty seconds of something I haven't seen since."

"And what was that?"

"You were sittin' under a tree in the backyard, pouring pellets into your air rifle—spilling most of them onto the grass, of course. Aw man, you were ready to shoot *something*. No, no. You weren't about to come inside unless you were holding something that once had a heartbeat or left a red trail from the pines to the patio. But there you stood, for hours, with a big pout on your face 'cause nothing passed your way. And then — *this* was the moment. A little sparrow—couldn't have been more than a few inches tall. You could have fit it in the palms of your little dirty hands. It hobbled right in front of you, it's little wings all mangled and torn."

"Oh, you're lovin' this," Ginger said.

"What did you do when you saw that bird?"

"Moses, I've got a race . . . we've got a race to get ready . . . "

"What did you do?"

Ginger paused before answering the question. He breathed heavy and could almost smell the sweet summer pine, Kool Ade Saturdays. The forgotten call of wind chimes.

"I cried," he mumbled, running a forefinger across his upper lip. "We got a damn race here, Mac."

Moses put the wrench down and ran a hand through the stray strands of his thinning hair, which backlit by a sole light bulb, looked like stalks of milkwheat sprouting from a lunar surface.

"Young Ginger Pervis. Champion of little broken things."

Ginger stared at the floor and watched the fading sun pull slivers of light across pools of oil.

Mel DeVaney rose to her feet with the rest of the crowd as Persy Higgins announced each driver over the intercom that was on loan from a local elementary school. Wiley Wiggins was a no-show. The word was that he was spending the night in jail for assaulting a man in his meat shop. According to derby-regular Lila Sturville, Wiley lept over the counter and beat a man half to death with a frozen cube steak. What the unidentified man did to provoke such a gratuitous outburst from the volatile Wiggins was unknown.

Mally beat her tiny palms together with each driver introduction.

And then she heard it. The most delicious sound in the world.

The El Diablo was rolling towards the starting line, its black bulk arched and quivering with anticipation. Moonlight streaked the hood and ignited a flash that rattled the rims of Mally's big brown eyes. There, mounted on the hood of the El Diablo, was what looked like a shiny silver angel, with her wings outstretched. Cadillac wings.

Mally's mouth trembled and went numb. She stopped clapping and held her shaking hands together under her chin.

Ginger looked at her and revved the engine, igniting a chorus of screams from the crowd.

"Well it looks like the Diablo means business tonight, Miss M," the elder DeVaney said in a half yell. She ran her hand through her daughter's hair, her fingers anticipating every slope and bump on her skull. At that moment Mel DeVaney's words and the wailing engines and the drunken crowd chants were drowned out by a singular sound that held the rapturous attention of Mally DeVaney's eleven-year-old ears—a sound that shook the roots of willow trees.

A sound that made a black bird with silver wings fly.

5

SECOND STREET

"It's a damn hot day," Big M exclaimed while straddling his three speed Schwinn in the alleyway between First and Second Street.

"Damn hot," repeated Little M, his nine year- old brother, standing beside him. Little M never really talked much until Big M spoke. Then he simply repeated in some form or fashion whatever this older brother said. Nobody really knew how the two brothers got to be known as Big M and Little M. The older brother was eleven, short and stocky while his younger sibling was tall and skinny. Their given names were Marvin and Theodore, respectively. Their mother called them Marty and Ted while their father succumbed to neighborhood tradition and referred to them as Big M. and Little M except when he was mad.

Then he simply bellowed their gender, "Boy."

The two brothers lived on Second Street, one of four streets that made up Magnolia Estates in the small South

Georgia town of Mulberry. It was a nice enough neighborhood although the six-room, shingle-sided tract houses
could hardly be called estates and no one ever remembered seeing a magnolia tree. Rumor had it that Hubert
Holbrook, the developer, did cut down two magnolia trees
that interfered with some road grading when he first started developing the neighborhood.

Magnolia Estates was referred to by real estate brokers
as a nice, middle class neighborhood. It was true that most
families who lived there thought of themselves as middle
class. In reality, except for First Street, everybody else was
on the low side of middle class. First Street was different. It faced the paved two-lane highway that connected
Mulberry with Newberry, twenty miles away. The people
who lived on First Street were honest-to-goodness middle
class although they thought of themselves as upper-mid-
dle class. Their houses were made of brick or wood siding
and had garages and brick barbecue pits. Two families
on First Street even had above-ground swimming pools.
Hot summer days found those pools full of yelling, splash-
ing First Street children, while their mothers sat in folding
chairs or reclined on beach towels trying to get the beginning of a tan before their annual three-day, Panama City
beach vacations. Second through Fourth Street children
were not invited. They had to settle for playing with a water hose, running through their Mom's sprinkler system,
or taking their chances in a nearby creek or fishing pond.
Maybe that's why on a humid night in mid-July, Big M and
Jimmy Simpkins, his best friend who lived on Third Street,

punched a dozen or more holes through each of the pools sidewalls while little M stood watch in the alleyway.

Big M, little M and Jimmy Simpkins were inseparable whenever they weren't in school.   There were three boys like all other nine to eleven year olds experiencing the long hot, slow summers of South Georgia. Whether sneaking around in someone's yard when the occupants weren't home or exploring the oak and yellow pine forests that surrounded them, each day was a new adventure. Had it not been for two inventions these three young boys and countless others like them would have perhaps, spent their summer days more productively.

The BB gun and the bicycle transformed young boys from the artistry of crayons and coloring books to marauding bandits, on the move and ready for action. With their three-speed Schwinns and Daisy rapid-fire, lever-action BB guns, Big M, Little M and Jimmy Simpkins defended their turf ruthlessly, especially when it came to any hapless kids who ventured from First Street. The streets were for cars and adults, but the alleyways were their domain, a kind of no-man's land fraught with danger and surprise attacks.

Leaning on his bicycle's handle-bars, Big M turned to his little brother and whispered, "I think I see Billy Ray Wilson. I bet he's gonna try and catch some minnows. Ride over to Jimmy's and the two of you meet me at the creek."

Little M nodded his assent with the seriousness of a special agent carrying out a dangerous assignment. He left in a cloud of dust, his skinny legs pedaling as fast as they could toward Jimmy's house.

Big M carefully loaded the BB's into his Daisy with delicate precision. His lips curled into a smile as he thought about his prey, Billy Ray Wilson, and the fun he and his compadres were going to have. Mr. big-shot, Billy Ray Wilson, was about to learn a thing or two. His fancy, chrome-fendered bicycle with the genuine leather saddle bags wouldn't do him any good when Big M and the boys got hold of him. It didn't matter if he and his chiropractor father, mother, and little sister lived in the biggest house on first street or not. When he used the alley or "thunder road" as Jimmy liked to call it, he was dead meat.

Big M wasn't really a bad kid. His parents' friends referred to him as a "spirited child." Adults who weren't acquainted with his parents called him a "little devil" or worse. In today's world a psychologist would probably describe him as an Attention Deficit-Hyperactive child. In the sixties there wasn't any Ritalin or related drugs, only keen switches at the hand of his mother to settle him down or a foot in his behind from his father to put the fear of the Lord into him. Big M once mentioned to his best friend Jimmy that he did not know the Lord well enough to be afraid of him, but he sure was afraid of his Daddy.

A bicycle, a BB gun and a couple of followers brought out the predatory instincts Big M possessed. He liked dangerous situations. The only thing he liked better than walking on the edge of danger himself was instilling fear and terror in others. Whatever the case, on that day, things didn't look good for Billy Ray Wilson. Big M's eyes narrowed as he chuckled to himself, peddling his bicycle ever faster toward the creek.

Billy Ray was bending over the creek, carefully working his minnow net through its waters when he heard the boys come up behind him. Big M stood in the middle of the path that led to the creek, flanked on both sides by Little M and Jimmy. Holding his Daisy air rifle in his left hand and wearing a pair of red-frame, superman sunglasses, Big M, who always had a flare for the dramatic, was more than a little cocky. Jimmy also looked confident, but not Little M. He shifted his weight from one foot to the other and held his BB gun as though he was afraid it might go off.

"Billy Boy, what do you think you're doing, riding down our alley and messing in our creek," Big M said in his most menacing voice.

"Yeah, who gave you permission, Silly Billy," chimed in Jimmy Simpkins.

"Yeah, Billy Boy," echoed Little M, who seemed to be gaining more confidence by the moment.

Billy Ray Wilson stumbled backwards, knocking over his minnow bucket. Beads of sweat began to break out on his forehead.

"I ain't doing nothing but trying to get me some minnows. This here's public property." Conjuring up all the false courage he could muster, Billy Ray continued, "It's a free country. My daddy said I could ride in the alley anytime I wanted to."

Big M inched towards Billy Ray, holding his air rifle with both hands. "Is that so, Billy boy? Your daddy's full of cow manure. He ain't even a real doctor."

"He is so a real doctor!" Billy Ray retorted, his red face raining sweat.

Almost in unison, Little M and Jimmy shouted at Billy Ray, "You're full of cow manure. Big M, let's make him eat boogers like we did last time!"

"Maybe later, but not just yet." Big M cocked his lever-action rapid-fire Daisy. "First, we need to teach Billy Boy a lesson for trespassing on our private property. "

Jimmy and Little M responded with a resounding "Yeah, that's right."

If Billy Ray Wilson had been raised differently and had not lived such a sheltered life, he would have realized that at twelve going on thirteen years of age, he was twice as big as any of the three boys confronting him. He could more than hold his own in a fight with any of them, but he didn't see himself that way. Inside he felt small and scared and wished he were home eating a Popsicle. All he could offer in his defense was a desperate, empty threat.

"I'll tell my daddy if you don't leave me alone."

As if on cue, Big M, Little M, and Jimmy Simpkins began laughing. Aiming his air rifle at Billy Ray's feet, Big M fired off a round and shouted, "Dance Billy Boy dance." And Billy Ray tried to do just that, but he really didn't know how. A second and third shot from Big M's Daisy kicked up little puffs of sand. The fourth shot hit Billy Ray in the left foot, stinging him through his black and white

Converse tennis shoes. Then he wet his pants and began to cry. More laughter and taunts of "Cry Baby" erupted from his three tormentors.

Suddenly, Billy Ray surprised everyone by jumping into the waist-deep creek where water moccasins had been spotted on more than one occasion and a mythical alligator was rumored to have eaten Arthur Johansen's poodle. He half-waded and dog paddled to the other side. Soaking wet, Billy Ray sloshed furiously through the blackberry bushes and brambles as fast as he could, running through the woods toward the safety of home.

"Let's catch him when he cuts through old Lady Fowler's back yard," shouted Big M as the three BB gun-toting marauders scrambled for their Schwinns.

Billy Ray ran hard and breathed harder, his water-logged sneakers squished their way toward First Street, while the predators pursued him in a cloud of summer dust. All four boys were sweating profusely --- one from fear and the others from the thrill of the hunt.

Everything in life depends on one's perspective. Leona Fowler and her friend Myrtle observed the chase on their way to the Shoe Mart's semi-annual sale in Newberry. The two women shook their heads with a certain disdain as they drove by in Myrtle's' Ford Fairlane.

Myrtle pursed her lips, "Leona, would you look at that? Those Jones boys and the Simpkins' son are chasing another boy."

Leona Fowler, a widow of ten years, had viewed similar incidents from her kitchen window and had dutifully reported each one in detail to her friends through extended party-line, telephone conversations.

With a disapproving tone, she replied "Doesn't surprise me a bit. Those second street hellions are always up to no good. I should know. They've trampled and torn up my flower beds more than once. The boy they're after is Billy Ray Wilson. His father is a professional Man."

To Leona and Myrtle, the event was a minor intrusion into their morning shopping spree, nothing more than a childish prank. To Big M, Little M, Jimmy and Billy Ray it was an epic struggle. As far as Billy Ray Wilson was concerned, he was literally running for his life. He remembered the booger-eating incident all too well, not to mention the BB gun induced dancing that comprised his most recent humiliation.

Billy Ray was a settler who had foolishly ventured too far from the safety of the fort and had been caught in a surprise attack with no means of defense. As he pushed his body to its physical limits, he promised himself that next time, he would pay more attention to his surroundings---if there was a next time.

To someone like Leona Fowler, Big M, Little M, and Jimmy were "hellions". To Billy Ray, they were worse than that; they were more like the devil incarnate. The three boys, however, saw themselves as heroes, protecting their homesteads from the carpet-bagging likes of Billy Ray Wilson and other First Street land barons.

Billy Ray almost made it, but not quite. Jimmy, the fastest rider of the three, cut off his escape route while Big

M and Little M surrounded him. Billy Ray, panting from the heat of a blistering hot Georgia sun, found refuge in Leona Fowler's metal utility building. He hunkered down in a back corner of the shed. The late Mr. Fowler's yard tiller and self-propelled lawn mower was all that stood between him and Armageddon. All he could do was clutch a broken-handled yard rake and shout over and over, "You better leave me alone!"

Meanwhile, Big M showed little M and Jimmy how to aim their air rifles at an angle so the BB's would ricochet off the walls and ceiling of the metal building. When one of the stinging projectiles found its mark, a yelp of pain from Billy Ray was their reward for persistence. After inflicting a barrage of BB gunfire, the three boys eventually became bored. Big M concocted a variation of their torturous game. Several times they rode down the alley, pretending to leave only to circle back and hide behind a nearby hedgerow. As soon as Billy Ray tried to emerge from the utility building, he would be met by a hailstorm of BB's from his well-concealed attackers, sending him back in full retreat to the rear of the building. Each time they pretended to leave he would wait longer before trying to make his get-away. Each time he was fooled and sent scurrying back into the building. The torment continued for almost two hours with no relief in sight when a miracle happened. Big M and Little M heard Miss Emma ring the dinner bell.

Even families on the back side of middle class could afford maids in the 1950s. Low wages and no benefits aside, even bad jobs were scarce for black women. The dinner bell rang a second and a third time. Big M and Little M looked at each other and smacked their lips. That sound could mean only one thing---chicken pot pies and maybe a little left-over peach cobbler for dessert. Chicken pot pies, four for a dollar at the local Winn-Dixie, were the hardtack and field rations of the fighting boys of Second Street.

Big M left Jimmy on sentry duty with strict orders: "Keep Billy Ray cornered until we return from lunch. Fire a few rounds ever so often to keep him trapped." No excuses would be accepted. Jimmy's reward for following orders would be that he would escape Big M's wrath and would be treated to some of Miss Emma's peach cobbler after they had completed their mission.

As always, Miss Emma's pot pies were superb. However, the peach cobbler was not to be. It had been requisitioned by the boys' father as dessert for his and their mother's evening meal. Big M and Little M would have to settle for a graham cracker to go with the last of their milk.

Wiping the cracker crumbs from his Batman tee shirt, Big M was none too happy about missing out on the peach cobbler. And as far as he was concerned, in a few minutes, Billy Ray Wilson was going to pay the price for that disappointment.

Full of chicken pie, graham crackers, and milk, Big M and Little M felt refreshed and re-energized. Mounting their trusty Schwinns, they were ready to return to battle. Little M carefully wrapped two graham crackers in a paper napkin and stuffed them in his tee-shirt. It wasn't the peach cobbler he had promised Jimmy, but it was better than nothing.

As Big M and Little M turned the corner toward Old Lady Fowler's yard, it was eerily silent. There were no sounds of BBs ricocheting off metal walls or taunts, or screams of pain---only a couple of blue-jays squawking and a dog barking in the distance.

"I don't like the sound of this," Big M grumbled, cocking his Daisy, " I don't like it one bit!"

"Where's Jimmy?" Little M whispered as he and his older brother surveyed their most recent battlefield, later referred to in various historical renditions as "Old Lady Fowler's building" or just the "Fight at Fowler's Place."

Their search first led them to the building itself, where there was no sign of Billy Ray or Jimmy. Their calls for Jimmy initially went unanswered. They found him sprawled on the ground, moaning and holding his bruised head, a casualty of a desperate counter attack.

Apparently Billy Ray Wilson had finally come to his senses. As confused and frightened as he was, he came to the conclusion that his chances, unarmed or not, were better against one than against three. His body, pumped up on adrenaline was more than ready for a dash to freedom. He was still afraid, but he sensed intuitively that his best chance for survival was to make his move.

At first he tried negotiating.

"Hey Jimmy, why don't you let me go?"

"No way," came the terse reply, followed by several quick rounds from Jimmy's air rifle.

The clock was ticking. It wouldn't be long before Big M and Little M returned and the torture resumed.

"Hey Jimmy, I'll give you my original Mickey Mantle baseball card if you'll let me go."

Billy Ray had upped his ante. He had gotten Jimmy's attention. The only thing Jimmy Simpkins liked as much as riding and shooting was playing baseball and collecting baseball cards.

Jimmy didn't answer right away. He was thinking the proposition over. Bribing one's guard to escape punishment is as old as history. Of course, Billy Ray Wilson had no intention of giving Jimmy his Topps Mickey Mantle card, but Jimmy didn't know that. He was considering whether or not such a rare treasure was worth Big M's wrath. Billy Ray was lying to Jimmy and Jimmy was wondering if he could tell a convincing lie to Big M. Absorbed with several possible scenarios, Jimmy laid his BB gun on the ground and began to rub his chin with his right hand, a nervous habit that signaled the rare occasion when he was trying to use his mind.

The distraction was enough.

When Billy Ray Wilson saw Jimmy drop his Daisy, every cell in his large body came alive in a spurt of self-preservation. From some former gene pool deep inside him emerged a blood-curdling rebel yell as he charged his tormentor. Eyes wide open with surprise, Jimmy reached for his Daisy and thinking better of it turned to run. Too late. Billy Ray lunged at him, half on purpose and half because he tripped over his size eleven tennis shoes. Whatever his intention was, the end result was that Billy Ray did a full belly-flop on Jimmy Simpkins. When they hit the ground, you could hear the air go out of Jimmy like a punctured birthday party balloon. Jimmy Simpkins lay in a crumpled heap on the ground, his right leg trembling uncontrollably. He wanted to cry, but first he had to get his breath. Realizing his advantage, Billy Ray picked up the air rifle. Holding the barrel with both hands, he pretended he was chopping wood on Jimmy's head. While Jimmy clutched his head and wailed in pain, Billy Ray took one last arching swing against a yellow pine, breaking the Daisy in two pieces.

Yelling "Home Run", Billy Ray Wilson ran victoriously toward the safety of First Street. His final action only increased Jimmy's agony, "You broke my gun, you broke my gun," he groaned between sobs.

Of course, the story Jimmy Simpkins told Big M when he arrived ten minutes later was slightly different. There was no mention of the Mickey Mantle baseball card or of Jimmy's inclination to abandon his post when Billy Ray charged him. As memory served him best, he stood his ground and after throwing several devastating punches was finally overwhelmed by Billy Ray's superior size. As best he could tell, he must have gotten knocked unconscious when Billy Ray hit him over the head with his air rifle.

To be fair, when Billy discussed the day's events with his chiropractor father, his memory proved to be selective as well. Forgotten were the dancing and wet pants or the crying and begging for mercy, and most certainly the attempted bribe. Instead, there was one against three--- good versus evil. It was high noon and Billy Ray was Gary Cooper. All he had were his fists against three punks with air rifles. Sure he got hit with several BB shots as his mother listened in horror. But then, no pain, no gain. He knew somehow he had to get to the ring leader of the Second Street terrorists. It wasn't Jimmy Simpkins that he disarmed and beat over the head with the assailant's own weapon. No, it was Big M himself.

"Big M!" his little sister exclaimed in awe.

Of course, it was Big M. After that, the other two fled for their lives.

As evening drew near, Big M, Little M and Jimmy Simpkins said their goodbyes before turning their bicycles homeward.

"Billy Ray Wilson better watch out," Big M imparted to his fellow marauders, "Tomorrow will be payback time."

Of course, everyday was payback time for somebody as far as Big M was concerned. And Billy Ray said pretty much the same thing as he finished his version of the day's battle. Rising from the dinner table with his father giving him a "that's my boy" smile, his mother still looking hor- rified, and his little sister beaming with a pride that could only come from having a big brother who had whipped the notorious Big M, Billy Ray's final words were: "All I can say is Big M and his two sidekicks better watch out if they cross my path again."

It should be noted that although both boys said pretty much the same thing, there was a certain distinction regarding the meaning of their comments.

Big M meant what he said and Billy Ray Wilson did not.

6

INVISIBLE BOY

Although wavy blond hair and clear blue eyes gave Teddy a strange sort of handsome, "five foot two, eyes of blue" was not a description that lived up to a teenage boy's testosterone dreams. To make matters worse, Teddy was not a particularly good name for a fifteen-year-old boy of slight build trying to prove his mettle in a one-street, blue-collar subdivision. And if his name and physique weren't enough of a handicap, his family's well-worn singlewide trailer stood out like a sore thumb in the sea of split-foyer, ranch and two-story stick built houses.

While the adults in the neighborhood weren't about to roll out the red carpet for the trailer family perched on a kind of no-man's land in a cornfield just on edge of the subdivision's boundary, they had just enough decency to accommodate to some extent, the family's lonely son.

Teddy's story was originally told to Little Jack, the neighborhood renegade and closest thing to a friend Teddy would ever have. His story filtered its way from Little Jack's parents to the Smiths then the Johnsons and on to the Bartholomews until everyone in the neighborhood had heard it at least twice, everyone except old man Murphy who stayed to himself in a vinyl-clad split foyer ever since his wife Norma died.

Of course, as Teddy's story made its way through the various families, it took on a number of twists and turns, exaggerations both added and subtracted. The gist of it is as follows: When Teddy was eight years old, his Daddy drank whiskey and beat and abused his mother while he and his younger sister were forced to watch. When in a drunken state, his father was fond of threatening to do his mother, sister and himself in with his good friends, Smith and Wesson. Weary of his relentless abuse, Teddy's mother decided to turn his father's friends against him.

Three times these friends spoke his name and three times stunned, he watched the red, concentric holes appear on his mid-section. He only uttered one word during the entire ordeal and he only said it once. After the first shot rang out, he shouted, "Teddy!"

Teddy and his sister looked on in silence as their father fell against the living room wall and slid down it, clutching what was left of his Bud-Lite and watching its contents mingle with the blood pouring from his belly onto the shag carpet.

Two years later, Teddy's mother married his current stepfather and two years after that they moved onto no-man's land.

Although Teddy and his mother had never spoken of the killing, and as much as he believed in his own mind that his father deserved what he got, one thing had always bothered him about the incident. He didn't like the way his dying father spoke to him. He didn't like being called by name as if he were some kind of official witness—as if he could have done something about the shooting. If Teddy hadn't been called out by his dying Daddy, he could have remained invisible. Of course, to the parents in the neighborhood, he was still for the most part invisible, but not so much that they wouldn't invite him in when he knocked on their front doors looking for refuge and a prospective playmate.

Still, the welcome mats, one after another, were eventually withdrawn because Teddy—like anyone dying of an unquenchable thirst—couldn't stop drinking from any sign of friendship and kindness that was offered, no matter how small or fragile. So on he went, from one house and playmate to another. As he searched for the next sign of hospitality, what he left behind looked like a clear-cut forest. Whatever his circumstance, no matter how many doors were closed to him and how few were open, there was always one place Teddy was accepted or at least tolerated—the basketball court at the end of the street.

In the cul-de-sac on Muskgrove Lane, a portable basketball goal and backboard stood guard like a silent sentinel and waited. Around three-thirty each fall afternoon, Monday through Friday, you could hear it coming before you saw it. An ancient yellow school bus slowly belched its way down the single curved road of Muskgrove Lane and expelled its prisoners, free until 6:45 the following morning.

They came out of that bus like rats leaving a sinking ship—first grade through high school. The youth of the neighborhood sauntered and ran toward the houses that beckoned them with the promise of snacks and juice. Thirty minutes later, the rhythmic thumping of basketballs sounded like a war chant and signaled that the games were about to begin.

Younger boys watched older ones dribble basketballs between their legs, make fancy lay-up shots and attempt the occasional but rarely successful, dunk. Boys and the several girls who braved the hallowed court raised their hands and voices, begging to be picked. But their cries to be chosen fell on deaf ears. To the older boys of Muskgrove Lane, they had been designated the Peanut Gallery, spectators one and all—spectators not players. Nothing more needed to be said. The best the members of the Peanut Gallery could hope for Monday through Friday was the brief window of opportunity that presented itself between games. Their reward for being loyal and appreciative spectators was the possibility of five minutes of wild abandon on the court while the real players took a water break at the end of each game. The brief melee only faintly resembled the game of basketball.

Although Teddy was old enough to qualify as a real player, he wasn't chosen—partly because of his questionable athletic skills, but most importantly because of his penchant for combing his hair when he was supposed to be guarding a player from the opposing team. Every few minutes, Teddy would reach for the comb protruding from his back pocket. It was like a personal hygiene compulsion. Teddy would raise his left hand in defense while he carefully manicured his blond tresses with his right hand.

It is no secret that one-armed basketball defenders don't fare well when their opponent dribbles past them while they are in mid-stroke for an easy lay-up. And no amount of laughter and derision from the older boys seemed to deter Teddy from his compulsion. So he was exiled Monday through Friday to the Peanut Gallery where he could comb in peace.

There was also one other more subtle, unspoken reason why Teddy wasn't picked to play in the real games. Technically, he wasn't a member of Muskgrove Lane and since it was important to many of the adults in Muskgrove Lane that Teddy and his family knew their place, it was also important to their children. The one exception was Little Jack. As the neighborhood rebel, he stood on more than one occasion as Teddy's sole defender. Although he was smaller in stature than Teddy, he was a fierce competitor on the Court and was known for starting fights that he knew he couldn't win.

Most of the boys in Muskgrove Lane, younger and older, were not inclined to rile up Little Jack because of his volatile nature, but even Little Jack couldn't get Teddy out of the Peanut Gallery. His one vote simply wasn't enough and besides, he didn't really want Teddy playing on his team. On Monday through Friday Teddy couldn't play, he could only watch, but on Saturday, things were different.

On Saturday, Detective Burns played. He was the only father in the neighborhood that was a Saturday regular. While the other fathers cut their grass, fished and golfed, Lloyd Burns played basketball with a bunch of kids. In fact, his wife, Myrtle, on more than one occasion indicated to the Detective that he was nothing more than a big kid himself. Of course, her comments went in one ear and out the other. While Lloyd loved his wife dearly, as far as sports were concerned, Myrtle definitely belonged in the Peanut Gallery.

All the kids and teenagers of Muskgrove Lane referred to Detective Lloyd Burns as "Sarge" in deference to his slight limp, the result of a wound he received in Vietnam and for which he received a Purple Heart. In truth, Sarge was admired not so much because he had received a combat medal or was a Police Detective, but because he could dunk the basketball with either hand whenever he felt like it. He designated his trademark dunk as the "Muskgrove Megadunk" or "M and M" for short.

Although he was judicious in its use, he always demonstrated the "M and M" once or twice each Saturday to the squeals and delight of the "Peanut Gallery." On Saturdays, Sarge was also the Team Captain and Referee.

More importantly, he always made sure everyone got to play. His authority and skill were unquestioned.

Sometimes Sarge's team would win and sometimes it wouldn't, but to the bewilderment of the older, more talented players, Sarge always chose the same person first to be on his team. He always chose Teddy. The Monday through Friday spectator was always the first one chosen on Saturday by the neighborhood Superstar.

Sarge's only requirement was that Teddy hand over his comb for the duration of the morning's activities. The older boys looked at each other and shook their heads in disgust as Teddy proudly took his place beside Sarge at Center Court. No one ever knew why Sarge always chose Teddy first. Teddy imagined that Sarge saw some hidden talent in him that wasn't apparent to the others, but then Teddy had always had a vivid and overactive imagination.

Sarge was every bit the Field General on Saturday mornings, preferring to pass the ball and set picks for his younger teammates from the Peanut Gallery. And the Monday through Friday All-Stars knew if they got too rambunctious or aggressive with Sarge's teammates, they would end up eating one of his "M and M's." Sarge would bark orders to his charges as if they were on a do or die combat mission.

"Teddy, guard your flank! PJ's moving to your right!"

"Hands up, Joey!"

"Defense team, Defense!"

"Shoot, Susie, Shoot!"

On Saturdays, the bonds of oppression were cut loose and the spirits of the weekday underclass soared. They imagined they were also players. When the lucky shot was rewarded with the swoosh of the net, they could count on a smile and a wink from Sarge.

"Money in the bank," Sarge would reply, giving the one who scored a "high-five."

On Saturdays, Teddy most of all, came alive for a few hours. On that day, he stood in the light and heard the applause and was called by his name. Unfortunately, Saturday only came once a week. There were six other days in between.

Then one Saturday, Teddy began to change.

Everyone had headed toward home except Sarge, Teddy and Little Jack. Sarge decided that the two of them needed some extra help with their free-throw shooting.

"Hey Sarge, Teddy says he's gonna become a Ninja," Little Jack commented as he threw up another errant free-throw.

"That so?"

Sarge gathered up the rebound and passed the ball to Teddy.

"Yeah," chortled Little Jack. "Teddy's done ordered his uniform."

Teddy bounced the basketball two times, and then swished it through the net.

"That so, Teddy?" Sarge queried, throwing the basketball to Little Jack.

Teddy pulled his comb out of his back pocket and began to run it through his hair.

"Yes Sir, Sarge. I'm gonna earn my black belt in Ninja."

Sarge leaned back against the pole that held up the backboard.

"Teddy, how you gonna do that—become a Ninja?"

Teddy's eyes lit up in a way Sarge had never seen before. His enthusiasm drew in Little Jack as well. It was like Teddy had found something important that he had been looking for and had eluded him until now.

"I ordered me a Ninja black belt training course from the International Ninja Training Academy for two hundred dollars. It took all my savings, but it'll be worth it. And they included the uniform for free!"

"That so?" Sarge grunted.

"Yes Sir."

"After I complete six lessons and send them in to Master Nu, he'll send me my Black Belt and official Certificate of Graduation."

Although Sarge showed little hint of his approval or disapproval of Teddy's venture, his eyes smiled ever so slightly in response to Teddy's excitement.

"Teddy, why do you want to become a Ninja?"

Without hesitation, Teddy revealed his plan.

"The thing about being a Ninja is that they teach you how to be invisible—you know—in a good way. You can sneak around and even though people won't know you're there, you can be on the look-out."

"Look out for what?" Sarge asked.

"Look out for any danger that might come their way so you can rescue them," Teddy replied somewhat impatiently.

"Your identity stays a secret. It's like you're a secret hero helping out people in trouble. Nobody might ever know the good you do, but at least you'll know. I'm gonna be like the invisible protector of Muskgrove Lane."

Sarge looked at Teddy and gave him a smile.

"Well Teddy, all I can tell you is that I'm glad there'll be a Ninja looking out for me in Muskgrove Lane."

That said, he picked up his basketball and began to walk toward home.

Looking over his shoulder, he shouted, "See you boys next Saturday."

As the years passed, Muskgrove Lane, like all neighborhoods, endured the usual timeworn transformations marked by the end of some things and the beginning of others. Seasons changed places, hairlines receded, and graduations brushed shoulders with first birthday celebrations. Even Jack shed the "Little" from his childhood moniker. On his fifteenth birthday, Little Jack made it clear that henceforth he would be addressed as "Jack." Anyone who referred to him as Little Jack would do so at his or her own peril, which translated into the teenage code of Muskgrove Lane as an "ass whipping." Occasionally adults slipped up and addressed him as Little Jack. When they did, he met their response with a cold stare and a stony silence. Only Teddy who had always been oblivious to neighborhood etiquette and traditions seemed able to get away with calling Jack, "Little Jack."

On a cool autumn afternoon Sarge spotted Teddy walking in the rain on the shoulder of Highway 87.

Sarge eased his Jeep Cherokee off the highway, rolled down the passenger side window and waited for Teddy. Within several minutes, Teddy peered in through the open window.

"Hi, Sarge."

"Hi, Teddy. How 'bout a ride home?"

"Okay. Thanks," Teddy replied easing himself into the back seat.

Lloyd looked at him in the rearview mirror.

"How's things going?"

Teddy didn't respond right away.

"Me and my stepfather ain't getting along too good. Never really have. He don't understand me. Guess it's hard to understand someone you don't much like."

Teddy's eyes met Lloyd's in the rearview mirror, then he looked out into the rain.

"I don't know what's gonna happen."

The Jeep Cherokee came to a stop where the gravel road began that led to the house trailer.

Lloyd put the gearshift lever in park and turned to Teddy.

"Teddy, whatever happens, I want you to remember something."

"Remember what, Sarge?"

"That you're a good boy."

"You really think so?"

"I know so, Teddy," Lloyd replied.

The corners of Teddy's mouth curved in the hint of a weary smile. He didn't quite believe what Sarge said, but appreciated the gesture nonetheless.

Getting out of the Jeep, Teddy closed the door and peered through the passenger window.

"Thanks for the ride, Sarge."

"Anytime, Teddy."

Lloyd listened to the gravel crunch grinding beneath his wheels as he pulled away from Teddy. He turned his head to look back. He could, just for a moment, barely make out Teddy, climbing his driveway with the heavy uncertain feet of an old man.

Time moved on. Like most people, the residents of Muskgrove Lane were preoccupied with the busyness of their lives—births, funerals, weddings, graduations and everything that went on in between. Jack and the others graduated from high school and then went off to college, work or wherever else their dreams and fears led them. The basketball court in the cul-de-sac looked lonely, having to settle for sporadic contests of "Horse" or "21." The glory days were gone and like all holiday seasons, Detective Lloyd Burns was overworked and underpaid.

Staring out of his office window and finishing the last of his stale, lukewarm cup of coffee, Lloyd watched the snowflakes float by in the dusk of evening. For police officers and detectives, Christmas wasn't particularly merry. When the phone rang at the precinct station, it wasn't to announce that Santa was passing out gifts, but more likely that he was passed out in an alleyway downtown. For the men and women of Precinct 44, Christmas was a time of drunken domestic squabbles, traffic accidents initiated by harried, preoccupied last-minute shoppers and barroom brawls where patrons, not reindeer, sported red noses. Lloyd chuckled softly to himself.

" 'Tis the season to be jolly."

"Hey, Lloyd, Officer Klein wants to see you down at Intake," bellowed McGillicutty, the burly Desk Sergeant.

"What does she want?"

McGillicutty looked up from the mound of paperwork on his desk and scowled.

"Hell if I know. What do I look like, a damn encyclopedia!"

Lloyd Burns looked at the clock. Ten minutes to quitting time. He grabbed his briefcase and ambled down the hall to the Intake room where he found Patrol Officer Susan Klein thumbing through a dog-eared card file.

"Susan, what can I do for you this fine evening?"

"Probably nothing. I thought I'd give you a head's up on a young guy we just picked up on a solicitation and drug possession charge down in the "fresh meat" district. Said he knew you."

Lloyd's heart sank.

"What's his name?"

Officer Klein flipped through the paperwork on her desk

"Let's see—here it is. He goes by the name Teddy Runion."

Lloyd took a deep breath.

"Yeah, I know him. What's the deal on him?"

Scrutinizing her report, Officer Klein talked as she read.

"Looks like it's his third arrest. Twice for prostitution and once for drugs. He's currently on probation which more than likely will be revoked, and since he's just turned eighteen, he may buy some time."

Rubbing his chin, Lloyd stared at Officer Klein.

"How 'bout diversion programs? Teddy was a good kid. Grew up in my neighborhood. He had a tough life—not many breaks."

"Yeah, didn't they all," Klein said as she neatly stacked the arrest reports.

"You might try Chris Smith's half-way house over in Chillicowee. He runs a good program. Better than most. A lot of his kids seem to make it."

"Thanks, Klein. I'll check it out. And thanks for the heads up."

"Don't mention it."

Lloyd called his wife as he had done so often before and begged off the Christmas party at her sister's. Having been a police officer's wife for twenty years she understood, but still found it difficult to mask her disappointment. Although he wasn't sure why, Lloyd didn't tell her about Teddy. There would be time enough for that later.

Lloyd spent the next two and a half hours making calls. Two programs turned him down and a third put Teddy's name on a waiting list. Finally, Chris Smith returned his call. Mustering up the last of his day's energy and stopping just short of begging, Lloyd gave Chris his best shot.

There was a long pause on the other end of the line.

"Okay, Detective. It must be the Christmas spirit. I'll find a way to make room for him. Bring him by tomorrow morning."

"Thanks, Chris. I owe you."

"Yes, you do Detective. Yes, you do."

The good news seemed to refresh Lloyd as he sauntered back down to Intake. He allowed himself a small smile and imagined that this could be the life-changing break that Teddy needed.

Lloyd looked through the interview window at Teddy. He had changed. His blond hair was still meticulously combed, but his face had a drawn, gaunt look to it. His left arm sported a tattoo of an angel.

Lloyd opened the door and walked inside.

"Sarge!" Teddy exclaimed, standing up and extending his hand.

"Hi, Teddy. Long time no see."

Teddy rubbed one eye and kept the other fixated on the badge clinging to Lloyd's coat pocket. "It really has been," he said, nodding to intensify his delivery. "Been a long while. How you doing?"

Teddy stopped rubbing his eye and smiled.

"I've had better days—worse ones too."

Lloyd nodded to an invisible beat and tapped on his coffee cup, his mind scrambling for words.

"Teddy, you know you don't have to live like this. I have friends who could find you a place at a half-way house. There are drug treatment center options, counseling—anything you need."

Teddy's face softened, his eyes a little less shaded.

"Sarge, I really appreciate you trying to help me," he said, "but the truth is, I don't want to change."

Lloyd leaned in closer.

"You sure? 'Cause I really want . . . I really do know some folks who can help you."

Teddy's face looked older, lines and creases sculpted by long walks up a gravel driveway.

"Yeah, Sarge," he said, "I'm sure."

Lloyd Burns tried, but couldn't hide his distress. He felt like he had been punctured with a giant pin and all the air had been sucked out of him. He tried to give Teddy a smile, but only partially succeeded so instead, he patted him on the shoulder and motioned to Officer Klein that he was through. As she led Teddy out of the office, he turned and looked at the Detective.

"Hey Sarge, you remember that time you gave me a ride home in the rain?"

Lloyd looked up and nodded his head.

"You said I was a good boy. I've never forgotten that."

Sitting in silence, Lloyd cradled his coffee cup in his palm and watched Teddy disappear down the hallway.

7

THE CRACKER JACK GOSPEL

His scarecrow-thin frame silhouetted by a dying sunset, seventeen-year-old Stanfield Huggins sprawled out in a close-cropped thatch of field grass, just beyond the pale reach of the only working headlight on his 1955 Chevy. A loaded .38-caliber pistol rested on his chest, and a sky full of stars, sparkling like flecks of rust in a moonshine still, filled his eyes.

An old sun-faded billboard advertisement for Chesterfield King Cigarettes loomed above him, its façade now serving as prime graffiti real estate for local spray-can assassins.

Stanfield stood up slowly, struggling to maintain his balance, and retrieved a Mason jar half-full of white grape juice from a pocket on his photographer's vest – a birthday gift from his uncle Lonnie, associate senior image consultant at "Smilz 4 Less" photo studio at the Baron Bend Mall outlet in nearby Ocala. Stanfield unscrewed the lid and stole two sips while walking toward the Chevy, its steady baritone rumble the only interruption in the evening's stillness.

Fireflies blinked in the cool autumn air and Stanfield traced "Sweet '73" insignia on the car's hood with his finger as he walked by. Decades ago, the moniker had been hand-stenciled by Stanfield's father, Silas, who at one time indulged in a weekend ritual of challenging other muscle car gearheads for weekend beer. Though having a thicker wallet by night's end was always a welcome reward, the more immediate pay-off for Silas and the other local white-line junkies was distraction from the sticky summer malaise that could canvas and cocoon a small county like Laramie.

It was a widely-held belief that in the era of Silas Huggins, nothing could touch the '55 Chevy: Not Bigsby Tuffard's '69 Charger Supreme, not Charlie Leffler's modified Mach I, not even Woodrow McIllvain's Supercharged Camaro SS (though that particular match-up stirred up a hornet's nest of debate for decades, from dive-bars to fellowship halls).

Long after Silas retired the '55 from the backroad racing circuit, Stanfield's older brother, Reginald, added the coup de grace to the car's mystique: a simulation of the Vietnam War's Tet Offensive, staged on the Chevy's sun-warped dashboard, using miniature green plastic army figurines. Though the installation earned Reginald lifetime revocation of all rights to drive the car, the elder Huggins ultimately left the scene-in-miniature intact as a tribute to his eldest son, after he was killed during his second tour of duty in Iraq. Following Reginald's death, Silas wanted little to do with the car – or, for that matter, his youngest son, Stanfield.

Taking one more sip from the Mason jar, Stanfield placed the container on the middle of the dashboard battlefield and slipped the pistol into one of his vest pockets. Across the road, the Three Kings Gas-N-Gulp – a family-owned outpost popular with teenage hot-rodders and methamphetamine runners – rested on a curvy hip of one of the area's most infamously gnarled and ornery two-lane veins – Route 77. The humble building looked like a model train set miniature against the high-rise backdrop of the Blue Ridge Mountains, now spackled with the comforting glow and blink of distant lights.

Stanfield's shy disposition, stick-thin frame and premature male-pattern baldness, which accelerated when he turned 16, ensured that his passage from puberty to young manhood in a rough-hewn mountain farming community would be rife with every imaginable mode of psychological, physical and social torment. And it followed him everywhere, from the doorstep of his home, to daily school bus rides – to the stale metal catacombs of the high school boys' locker room, where he had found himself, only hours earlier in the day, introduced to a brand new discourse in humiliation. A teenage brood, featuring a smattering of Napier Street Baptists' finest senior Youth Ambassadors, pinned Stanfield's naked wisp of a frame on the locker room shower tile floor and tattooed, with a makeshift kit, "Pigeon Shit Bombb Zone" on his bald pate.

The local artisan whose handiwork now graced Stanfield's thin-to-gone crown was Simms Clearwater, a wiry, flame-haired juvenile hall regular and infamous schoolyard terrorist. This particular evening announced Simms' debut weekend working the night shift solo at the Three Kings Gas -N-Gulp, and for Stanfield, that meant only one thing: Simms Clearwater had to die tonight.

Stanfield slipped out of the Chevy's driver-side door, brisk-ly made his way across the two-lane stretch and stumbled onto the Three Kings parking lot. The gravel crunch beneath his boots sounded off like miniature demolition explosives, and he turned to look back at his car, its idling engine grumble still audible from a distance. Nearing the storefront, his footsteps slowed to a creep, and he scanned with nervous eyes the old two-lane, snaking off into the darkness, determining that the anonymity of his mission was secure. Picking up speed to a slow jog (made awkward by his prominent limp, a birth defect doctors had never been able to rectify), Stanfield passed by Simms' mint green low-rider truck, its rear bumper bookended by two stickers that read "Draggin' ASSphalt Kustom Society."

He paused in front of the store entrance, his mouth dry and a hornet's nest hum ringing in his ears. He felt nausea climbing from his stomach to his throat, and gripping the store entrance door so tight his fingers ached, Stanfield willed himself inside, a trio of bells signaling his arrival.

The store was filled with an eerie calm – only the random hiss of carbonation pumps nestled near the soda fountains punctured the silence. His heart beating jack-hammer loud, Stanfield approached the end shelf of the store's magazine stand and gripped it with both hands, his chest heaving in short intense intervals. He noticed an issue of *Men's Health* magazine had been opened to a dog-eared page advertising "male enhancement" pills, and he startled himself by letting loose a muted snicker. Scanning an aisle of random shrink-wrapped offerings, Stanfield placed a hand on his increasingly nauseous stomach. Colors and contents began to blur and pulse. He exhaled deeply, wiped a patch of sweat from his brow and reached for a bag of Cracker Jacks, his brother Reginald's favorite snack.

When his brother was in Iraq, Stanfield would send him each month a personalized stash of Cracker Jack boxes – along with a narrated recording of the latest town news and gossip, and a stack of *Famous Monsters Of Filmland* magazines (a passion the two brothers shared in secrecy). Without fail, Reginald would send a return letter each month containing the prize from each Cracker Jack box. Stanfield kept every one of those prizes – 25 in total – and stored them securely in the Chevy's glove compartment (and every single morning before school he counted the small square treasures to make sure they were all present and untouched.)

The task at hand abruptly shoved its way back to the front of his mind, and Stanfield closed his eyes, his breathing now slightly more manageable. He settled his hand on the cool steel of the pistol, its bulk feeling heavier in his hand than he remembered. A dull throb commandeering his skull, and an intensive series of quick, shallow breaths escaping his lungs, Stanfield gritted his teeth, slipped his trigger finger in place, and began to accelerate around the aisle-corner ice cooler display, his head a storm of feelings both fearful and enraged. But as he rounded the corner, he found his path obstructed by the long, crumpled frame of Simms Clearwater, slumped haphazardly like a ragdoll. His thick freckled arms, stained with cheap tattoos, were folded across his lap, and his back leaned awkwardly against a Trident Gum display rack. A thatch of mostly empty Budweiser bottles took up residence near his left hip. Others, with the labels peeled off, had either tipped over or rolled away, just outside his reach.

Stanfield stood frozen, his finger now sweating against the trigger; his aching knees a body's length from his intended target.

"My Daddy's dead," said Simms, his words a slurred whisper, tinged with a child-like cadence, his grief-smeared eyes slowly rolling side to side. "They told me he collapsed in the fruit aisle at the Piggly Wiggly half an hour ago."

Stanfield felt like he was separating from his body, only anchored to the moment by an ache growing in his grip.

"Betty Bivins had been talking to him," Simms continued, his raw eyes rolling over white. "She said he just stopped and looked at her for a second, and said: *'Well. Ain't that something.'* Then she said he fell to the floor, spilling apples everywhere. Said they rolled all over the damn floor and just kept goin', kept rolling – and before they stopped, he was gone."

Shaking his head, Simms bit his lower lip so hard a trickle of blood began to form. A fresh flood of emotion rushed across his face.

"He don't even like apples," he said. "Nobody in my family does – except for me. Ain't that something?"

Simms formed the shape of a gun with his right hand and pressed the barrel finger against his temple. "I swear to God, if you had a gun on you, I'd ask you to shoot me *right Goddamn now*," he said, his face distorted by grief.

Stanfield loosened his grip on pistol in his pocket and interlocked his fingers on top of his head, his eyes squeezed shut. He could feel the newborn scabs taking shape on his scalp, as well as additional residue from the morning's brutal episode.

Making a feeble attempt to sit up, Simms wiped his face with his shirtsleeve and stretched for one of the few remaining open bottles of beer.

"My Daddy was a barber at the Cut & Dried shop on Bartlett Avenue," he said, "and he always cut my hair the first Saturday of every month." He took a deep pull from the bottle and rubbed the red-hued burr of his scalp, his words trailing off. "Do you know what the three stripes on the barber pole stand for?"

"No, I don't," Stanfield answered, his face colorless, his eyes now wide and wired.

"Each color means something different," Simms continued in a slurred monotone, as if repeating a pamphlet slogan he had been familiar with his whole life. "The red means blood, the blue represents a person's veins…and the white represents bandages used to wrap folks up when they get cut. My Daddy taught me that.

"I always thought my momma was the blue – she gave us life. I was the red 'cause I always came home bloody from somethin' or another. But my Daddy was the white. He always put everything back together again – cleaned the wounds. But now…"

Simms slammed the back of his head against the display rack, his light blue eyes suddenly vacant and his lower jaw hanging open.

Stanfield stood quietly and began to open up the box of Cracker Jacks he had been holding in his pocket. After a few short seconds of digging around the box's contents, he retrieved a thin, small square of paper. Holding it between his fingers, he carefully leaned forward and placed it at Simms feet, then began a slow shuffle toward the exit door.

Simms, still bleary eyed, managed a few words between hoarse dry heaves of emotion.

"What's this?"

Stanfield rubbed his eyes, exhausted.

"For a long time, it was what I used to stop the bleeding," he said. "But I think you need it more than me tonight. I'm sorry for your loss."

Stanfield walked back to the Chevy, its engine still idling steady and strong. He removed the pistol and slipped it beneath the rear bench seat. Looking at the glove box, he paused for a moment before opening it. Inside was a small cedar box containing 25 neatly stacked Cracker Jack prizes. Stanfield counted each one of them, put the box back in the glove compartment, and felt his eyelids grow heavy to the V8 engine's lullaby hum.

8

TIN SPOKE PARADE

Through a torn strip in his screen door, on a night when silver sheets of rain fell heavy and hard as fists, LeeRon Free watched Alva King's only child, Critter, disappear forever. The fierce pounding of rain on metal roofs drowned out the sound, leaving only the sight of a police officer struggling with his footing as he tried to restrain Alva. Her housecoat was soiled by the mud and her eyes rolled back in her head as her arms desperately flailed about, reaching out for her son.

Bathed in a blue and red flicker of light, two other officers dragged Critter through the mud, his imposing frame stubborn and slippery.

Grabbing the rear bumper of the police car, Critter heaved twice, and threw up, giving the two weary officers enough time to cuff the boy's thick wrists. One policeman finished restraining him while the other bent over to catch his breath and picked up his hat.

Looking through the slit screen, LeeRon turned his eyes and caught a glimpse of his son, Augustus, standing on the edge of the front porch steps. He stood there motionless, a spindly shadow, small against the rain, and watched the cruiser disappear into darkness, pulses of light fading in its wake. Augustus turned to look back at the screen door, his eyes meeting his father's through the torn slit.

"Police lights look pretty in the rain, Daddy."

The morning sun wiped the sky clean of clouds and Augustus sat on the only patch of grass decorating the front yard. The soft, cool blades felt good against his bare legs. LeeRon watched his son through the tear in the screen door, his eyes still feeling the ache of flashing red & blue lights. The distance between him and his son was only a few feet, but what divided them was something more profound. LeeRon lit up a cigarette and observed his son hoisting up his socks above his kneecaps.

The socks. He never understood the socks. Long, thick yellow wool socks. Augustus wore them almost every day.

"You look like a bumblebee with them socks, boy," LeeRon blurted out, a throaty laugh escaping his chest. "Ain't no black boy in his right mind wear them things, young 'un."

Augustus stood up and looked at his father, his eyes burning so far back in his head they seemed to disappear.

"Ain't no bumblebee," he said. "A hornet."

"A what?"

"Hornet. When a bumblebee sting you, it ain't nothin'. When a hornet sting you, you know you been stung."

A smile split across LeeRon's broad face. He flicked the ashes from his cigarette and picked at the torn slit in the screen door.

"Today's the day, itn't it."

"Schwinn Stingray. Yalla. 26 inches. Ape hanger handlebars. And tassels on 'em. Red, white & blue. They come extra, but I had some money left, so I said, 'put 'em on'."

Augustus never had much to say, but often when he'd talk, it would come out in a heap—and fast, as if the words bandied together because they were afraid to step out alone. Augustus looked up at the sun and plucked at his hair.

"You got your money for Mr. Weston?"

"Yessir."

"You know what my daddy used to call money?"

"Nosir."

"Cooked greens."

Augustus smiled, patting his shorts pocket again. LeeRon smiled back. His eyes traced the contours of his son's face, and he thought about how thankful he was to watch in real time what he could only imagine just months before, at least until that crisp March morning, when he had watched the words "State Correctional Facility" disappear into the rearview mirror of his brother's Chrysler LeBaron. He still kept in his pocket a folded piece of toilet paper from the prison with two objectives written on it: Augustus and homemade cornbread. A three-year stint in the confines of brick and steel had wounded some things inside LeeRon Free, but not the memory of Augustus' smile. It was brighter than the sun. Brighter than yellow wool socks in the summertime. LeeRon hoped every time his son smiled, it would take in some of the slack between them. The memory of Augustus' mother was still fresh, and LeeRon knew he was going to have to sew up the wound stitch by stitch.

The elder Free's 38-year-old bones strained and ached as he sat down on his front steps, reminding him of the overtime he agreed to work at the cotton mill later that afternoon.

"C'mere, bumblebee, I want to show you something," LeeRon said, stealing a quick draw off his cigarette.

Augustus walked up rotted wood steps and sat down next to his father. A long blue car, loud muffled music thumping from the inside, rushed by in a blur, catching Augustus' attention.

"Hold out your hand," LeeRon asked, holding out his own hand as an example.

Augustus followed suit.

"You know how a bumblebee flies to the sky?"

"No sir."

"Like this, now hook your thumb around my thumb and do what I do." LeeRon put out his cigarette in an old can next to the stoop and began moving his hand like a flapping wing, his own thumb hooked around his son's. "Now you do it."

Augustus began moving his hand in the same motion, eventually getting in synch with his father's movements. The two sat in silence for a long moment.

"A little blackbird," LeeRon said, nodding his head and smiling.

Augustus smiled and mouthed his father's words without saying them, his eyes fixated on the motion of their hands.

"Be careful on your way to town, little man, alright."

"Alright, Daddy."

"Maybe when you get back we'll go ridin' together."

Augustus nodded, hoisted up his sock and stepped out onto the sidewalk, his ears perked in anticipation of a kickstand squeak, his thoughts adrift on dirt roads, out there somewhere, awaiting adventure.

In the summertime, Gracious Weston would sit on the old blue metal chair out in front of her father's hardware store, Gracious Goodness, Inc., and wave at passersby. Sometimes they would wave back, but she liked it better when they honked their horns. Each time a driver obliged Gracious, she would clap her hands and look over her shoulder to see if her father was watching. Sometimes he would toss a glance her way and unbox a hurried smile.

"Grace, stay away from the street," he commanded, his voice reedy but firm.

"I'm not at the road," Gracious countered, clutching her raggedy stuffed animal, a butterfly named July, whose age and origin was unknown.

"Listen to me, lil' miss—keep your fanny away from the road."

Gracious kicked her tiny legs against the chair's sunburned metal seat and tried to slip her arms through the old dress she was wearing. She'd often do this in moments of frustration. The dress she wore this morning was from an old clothes rack keeping company with a collection of other unwanteds waiting out their sentence in the back of her father's store.

Gracious watched the heat rise off the empty cracked curve of pavement that hooked around the corner of the store. She held her necklace, a long length of dental floss strung with fruitloops, up to her nose.

She giggled as a stray summer breeze, unusual for that time of day, slipped through a gaggle of magnolia trees and bubbled under her dress. The wind whipped up with more ferocity, and Gracious covered her ears as a flock of motorcycles, roared around the hooked curve like a swarm of growling black beetles sparkling under the sun.

Slipping off her shoes, Gracious stood up on the chair and clapped twelve times.

Mint leaf patches edged the old dirt roads that sprouted from downtown. Augustus let their scent fill his nostrils as he trudged along an old mud-caked sidewalk toward the hardware store.

Augustus liked to wear his socks up to his knees, and his left sock always seemed to retreat during the summer, scrolling itself down around his knobby ankles. It would frustrate him to no end and he'd count the cracks in the sidewalk until it was time to kneel again and hoist up the yellow fabric.

A chorus of cicadas filled his ears as he stopped to look up at the sky. It was usually his tradition to seek out a few clouds, decide what kind of animals they were shaped like, and pretend they were having a conversation with each other. Once he imagined a rhinoceros engaged in a shouting contest with a salamander. But today, the sky was scraped clean by a blazing sun.

Feeling veins of sweat attempting to surface, Augustus reached to pull up his sock and scratch his knees. Across the street, the parking lot for the Spray 'n' Sprint car wash wore the sad Saturday morning crown of gutted beer cans and anonymous paper bags.

Augustus would sometimes spend evenings beneath dusk's last light watching the old businessmen wash their Cadillacs. Occasionally, they'd even let him help, rewarding him with a couple of coins.

Percy Threece owned both the Spray 'n' Sprint and the adjoining Wing-A-Ding chicken wing shack, a hot spot that romanced the lunch crowd. Augustus enjoyed sitting on the curb, popsicle in hand—pineapple flavored, preferably—and watch the parking slots fill with cars. He would read the plates on the back of the cars that spelled out names like "POOKY" and "T-DAWG."

"Now, now, little brown cow, where you been?" asked Percy Threece, emerging from behind a large trash barrel, half eaten away by rust. "Haven't seen you for a long spell, youngblood."

Percy always carried a small transistor radio strapped on his wrist with a leather band branded with his initials, "P.T.T." Tapping his white leather shoes on the pavement, he twiddled a dial until settling on a station he liked.

"Ummhmmm," he softly uttered, his lips tucked in, eyes squeezed shut and hips swinging back and forth. "There it is, youngblood—there—it—is—M-A-R-V-I-N. Some folks go Mr. Mayfield as the soul of soul. I go Mr. Gaye. Others loved it, but he lived it, you see. That's the difference."

Augustus unveiled a polite smile and reached down to pull up his sock. As usual, he had no idea what Percy was talking about.

"Scraped me up 'bout ten bucks worth of scratch this mornin', young Augustine, St. Augustine the Explorer," Percy said. "Last week I only got about five. You never know when you gonna find the good stuff. Life's funny like that, I guess. You don't tell it, it tell you!"

"So where you headed?"

Augustus rubbed the back of his head and kicked a piece of gravel off the pavement. "Goin' downtown. To Gracious Goodness. Got me a bike on layaway and today's the day. A Schwinn 26 incher. A Stingray. Got a banana seat and handlebar tassels—red, blue and white. Like the flag but without the stars."

Percy reached down to pick up a quarter off the pavement. It was still wet from last night's rain. "Guess what year this is and you can keep it," he said.

Augustus squinted his eyes and clicked his teeth together several times before answering. "1967—the first year Schwinn made the Stingray. I'll go with that."

Percy looked at the coin intensely, the tip of his tongue peeking out from between tightly drawn lips. "Nope. But close enough."

He flipped the coin to Augustus, who snatched it from the air with his right hand, which both surprised and pleased him because he was left handed.

Percy wiped a dirt stain off his shoe, patted his sweating brow with a kerchief and shuffled closer to where the boy was standing. Augustus could see dark-lined folds of skin that barricaded the old man's eyes.

"A bike huh?" Percy asked, patting his forehead with the kerchief again.

"Yessir. A Stingray. Yalla."

"Goodness, now. Yalla? Like them socks you got on?"

"Yessir. Kind of."

"Everytime I see you St. Augustine, you got them yellow socks on. How come you don't wear no other color?"

"I don't like no other color."

"Fair enough, now youngblood, fair enough," Percy said, his words stuttered by soft laughter. "You a peculiar spoke, little man. We all spokes on the wheel, now, St. Augustine—you just sparkle a little more than most."

"You gonna give me a ride on that new bike of yours?"

Augustus skeptically cocked his head and scanned Percy's abundant midsection. "Think you can fit on my handlebars?"

Percy laughed out loud, the sounds cracked and raw from a lifetime love affair with cigarettes. "Your daddy know you this funny?"

Augustus bit at his lower lip and tugged at a loose thread hanging off his shorts. The sun pulled his shadow across the pavement. "My Daddy don't really know me too much. Things different since Momma died."

Percy switched off his radio and kneeled down beside Augustus, resting a hand on his tiny shoulder.

"Like you—like all of us—your daddy a spoke too, Augustus. He just beat up and bent a little. He's gonna need you to stand strong with him and keep that wheel rollin', alright?"

Augustus nodded once and looked back down at his shadow on the concrete.

Percy stood up and wiped his brow again.

Augustus pulled up his sock and waved goodbye.

"You the spoke that sparkles, baby boy," Percy yelled, watching the boy lope off toward the old sidewalk. "Keep that wheel turning."

The sun had its hot hand on Augustus' back, escorting him into town. He could see ghosts rise from the sweating pavement in the kind of summer haze that crept through towns on days like this, accompanied by the sounds of over-worked air-conditioning units about to rattle off their hinges.

Grady Street was Augustus' favorite route to take when visiting the Weston's store. He looked at the yards with old cars left to rot in beds of pine needles that lined the lawns, tucked away and strangled by kudzu. Sparks of sunlight would reflect off their hood ornaments, popping like camera flashes. Augustus would blow kisses to the large houses and pretend he was a movie star as he walked.

Up ahead in the distance, Augustus could see the hand-painted neon sign for Monk Theef's Rexall Pharmacy. He stopped to tie his shoe and picked up his pace a bit, his heartbeat pumping faster. He could almost smell the inside of the Weston's store, with its stacked bags of fertilizer cramped in the corners and the sound of the ceiling fans and the fresh peanut bin. In his mind Augustus was feeling the fresh rubber bike-tire tendrils between his fingers, and watching those handlebar tassels flicker, blown by the tabletop fan Mr. Weston had put there just for the effect.

A cigarette dangling between his lips and a bottle of beer clutched in his hand, Monk Theef stepped outside his store and watched young Augustus stop in the middle of the street and pull at his sock. He smiled to himself and shook his head.

"Bumblebee boy, what brings you to my humble establishment this morning?"

Augustus walked up to the telephone pole in front of Monk's pharmacy and linked his arms around it. "I ain't no bumblebee," he answered. "I'm a hornet."

Monk snorted and stroked the tight cornrowed strands of hair draping over his shoulders. "Well now, you know, bumblebees fly close to the ground, close to the flowers, where the sweetness is. That's where I see you, young 'un. Not in no hornet's nest."

Augustus looked up the telephone pole, squinting his eyes at the sun. "You ever climb this pole?" he asked.

"Sometimes."

"Why you do that?"

"Don't know for sure." Monk put his cigarette out on the pavement and took a swig from his near-empty bottle. "Guess when I'm up there, things look different," he continued.

Augustus' attention drifted down the street a couple of blocks where he could see Gracious Weston, keeping company with her chair in front of her father's store.

Peeking her head out of the dress in which she had cocooned herself, Gracious watched Augustus walking toward her and began to wave wildly. She leaped out of her chair, clutching her doll, and ran up to where the store's sidewalk met the road. She stopped and turned around to see if her father was looking, but he had disappeared to the back of the store.

"Hey Augustus," she said, her sweet south Georgia lilt welcoming, and her eight-year-old hands clapping together excitedly.

Augustus pointed at Gracious' ragdoll. "She need to be cleaned up," he said.

"July doesn't like baths," she replied, clutching the doll tight to her chest. "You want to hold her?"

Augustus was the only person Gracious would let hold July because she liked his soft hands and thought maybe her mother's hands would've felt like his.

Peeling off his shirt, Augustus took July in his arms, holding it like a baby, and dropped to his knees. He dabbled a corner of his shirt in a puddle of water next to the curb and began to wipe the patches of dirt off the doll's furry face. After a few more dabs he stood up, handed July back over to Gracious' anxious hands and slipped his shirt on.

"There, like new," he said. "A new July."

Gracious pressed the doll softly to her face as Augustus made his way into the store. Bundles of roofing shingles leaned heavy against the walls. He could feel the subtle breaths pushed down from the whirring fan blades above head. A couple of customers donning suspenders and caps pulled tight over their brows sifted through bins of nails and bolts with thick farmers' hands, weighing the merchandise on hanging scales.

His heartbeat thumping and his palms sweating with anticipation, Augustus reached deep into his pocket and pulled out the money necessary for his final payment. He held the crinkled bills between his short, small fingers and walked towards Mr. Weston's cash register. While carefully laying the bills down on the counter next to the register,

Augustus's attention got hijacked by the sight of clouds forming outside the store windows. Watching the shapeless puffs roll across the sky, he imagined a kangaroo riding on the back of a whale and smiled.

A few quiet moments ticked by and Augustus' attention was jostled away from the window pane by the sound of someone whistling. He followed the sound and it led him back outside to the front of the store where Zimmery King stood, smiling and holding up Augustus' new bike.

Augustus tugged at his socks as he ran towards it. Schwinn. Stingray. Racing yellow. Tasseled handlebars.

"Today's the day," Zimmery said, rubbing his hand over the bicycle's seat, still covered by factory plastic. Gracious was clinging to her father's leg, bending her fingers in gentle waving motion at Augustus. "You ready to ride young man?!"

"Yessir."

"Well why don't you tie those shoe laces and climb on top this hotrod. Looks like rain's comin'. You better get goin' so your daddy don't worry."

Augustus thanked Zimmery and waved goodbye to Gracious.

"This bike will be your wings, young man," Zimmery said as Augustus tapped his feet against the pedals and mounted the seat. "Fly high, young 'un!"

Pushing off from the curb, Augustus adjusted his feet to the pedals. He could hear the rattle snap of the bike chain adjusting to the gearshift and the hum of new tire rubber spinning against concrete. His heart soared.

Augustus accelerated and jumped the sidewalk curb, pedaling onto the curvy stretch of road that hooked around the Weston's store.

Wearing a smile brighter than Christmas, Augustus closed his eyes and imagined himself flying in the clouds, above everything. Above the police lights that gave his daddy headaches, above rusted tin roofs. Up in the clouds with the rhinoceros and the kangaroo, and the whale. Up high and free.

By the time LeeRon Free arrived at the corner block in front of Gracious Goodness, policemen had pushed most of the onlookers away, though the presence of their sadness lingered. A light rain had started to fall, and LeeRon was standing next to his son, lying still and broken on the concrete, his yellow socks tattered and torn.

Witnesses who watched the delivery truck round the bend said the boy never had a chance.

Gracious Weston was sitting next to Augustus' body, his head resting in her lap. She was using a torn strip of her dress to delicately wipe the gravel and blood from his forehead. LeeRon kneeled down and held his son's hand. Wet flashes of blue and red filled his eyes, changing places with each heartbeat.

Words and sounds were unable to battle their way from his throat as thunder boomed in mourning and retreated down the avenue. LeeRon hooked his thumb with his son's small hand and slowly moved his fingers together in the motion of a wing. An unexpected breeze blew through and lifted the red, white and blue tassel strands, still clutched by the boy's hand and carried them high into the pines across the street.

And for a few moments, a chorus of cicadas hushed in reverence.

9

SUNDAY BISCUITS

Mildred Percy stood at her kitchen window--the one decorated with ceramic thimbles donated by her third-grade Sunday school class--and watched the parking lot lights across the street snuff out one by one.

It was getting late.

She walked to the kitchen screen door, one hand caked in Bisquick and the other holding a bottle of sorghum molasses she had removed from the antique cupboard. Her husband, Elmer, liked biscuits for supper on Sunday evenings. He would often joke to his six p.m. Sunday night congregation that the evenings sermon may be cut short because it was biscuit night.

Tonight, though, it was getting late; the clock was creeping past eight-thirty.

"Elmer!" It's close to suppertime," Mildred shouted in a voice so loud it surprised her.

Five minutes ticked by and still no sign of her husband. She looked out at the old oak tree in the back yard, its branches lifted by a late summer breeze, as if it were shrugging its shoulders, saying, "I don't know where he is either." Mildred smiled at that thought for a quick moment and returned her attention to her missing husband. She knew he'd grunt and groan if the biscuits and sorghum weren't on the table by the time her grandmother's clock struck five o'clock. She didn't mind it so much – the biscuits, that is, not the clock. She had always hated the sound that clock made.

Slamming the screen door behind her, Mildred hurried to the garden where she found Elmer, crumpled on the ground, his legs spread and his back against the old oak. He was holding the gold office pen he always had clipped to his shirt pocket, the one she got him for Christmas, with his name engraved on it. His thumb was nervously clicking the pen.

"Mr. Percy, what in the world is going on with you. Those biscuits are gonna crawl back in the can if you don't come eat 'em!" Mildred arched her eyebrow in disapproval and placed her bisquick-caked hand on her hip, just like her mother used to do. She hated when her mother did that.

"Something happened to me Milly," Elmer said in a soft voice, wiping at eyes wet and raw with tears.

Mildred's wrinkled brow softened and she could feel her heartbeat begin to race. A warm breeze lifted the hair off her neck and carried with it the unmistakable scent of burning biscuits. She mourned them for a split second.

"Well Lord have mercy, do I need to call Dr. Elsey, or 911?" she asked her husband.

Elmer shook his head and ran his hand through the tall grass beside him. He bit his lower lip – a lifelong nervous habit of his – the words in his throat falling apart before making their way to his mouth. He breathed deeply and watched clouds move across the sky. He thought for a moment about how he had never noticed the sky before.

Mildred hesitantly took his hand. He could feel her worry moving over him.

"What's going on with you, Elmer Percy?" she asked with soft urgency. "You want to come inside and talk about it? Those biscuits are…"

Elmer gave her hand a slight squeeze and looked up at her.

"I think I had a dream."

"A dream? What kind of a dream?"

Elmer sighed and ran his hand through the grass again. He shook his head slowly, watching the sun drop a couple of rungs down the sky.

"Don't know," he answered. "I took a rest here at the oak for a spell after checking on the garden. Must've dozed off. Can't say for sure what happened after that."

He picked a hand full of grass and let it get swept up by a wisp of evening breeze.

Mildred breathed deep and picked at the dried biscuit mix on her hand. Some of it had gotten in her watch and she drew her lips tight in mild frustration. She liked that watch.

"You want to tell me what you dreamed?" she asked, rubbing her forehead with her clean hand. A few moments passed without an answer, and Mildred sat down in a thatch of tall grass beside her husband. She could feel his hand shaking.

"I guess so," he finally responded. "I'm not sure you'll understand, and…well, it's pretty crazy. I'm not sure I understand it myself. Must have been asleep, but –can't explain it– I felt…awake. More awake than usual. In the dream I was standing in this crowd of people – all kind of people, young, old, and folks our age. And they were laughing and carryin' on – and dancing. They were dancing to that rock and roll fuss that I used to say was the devil's dance and the reason deaf people never had it so good."

Mildred let slip a slight smile.

"Well, you can bet your biscuits I wanted to leave that place as fast as I could," Elmer continued. "But even though I wanted to leave, my feet wouldn't move."

He reached down and touched his ankle. Mildred's eyes followed his hand.

"The people looked so happy and then I noticed they were all looking at one person who was dancing and laughing with them. Then the person they were looking at looked at me, and…"

Mildred reached to touch her husband's temple, turned gray by two heart attacks, a wayward daughter and a few bad breaks that could have gone either way.

"Milly, this sounds awful crazy," Elmer said, shaking his head. "I just… ."

Elmer paused, his voice, the once-commanding baritone one would expect from a veteran preacher such as himself, disappearing into a hoarse, almost childlike whisper. It was a rare moment of vulnerability, and for Mildred, it did not go unnoticed.

She sat still in the tall grass that swayed side to side in the dying dusk light, holding her husband's trembling hand. Her eyes traced the old wrinkled lines and she thought about when those hands held their child for the first time, and how they helped bury her mother when she passed away from liver cancer, and how they could also be swift and fierce.

"Tell me what happened," she said, watching tears streak her husband's cheeks."

Elmer breathed deep and turned his head away from his wife, wiping his face. "Well, the person looking back at me was him."

"Him who?"

Elmer's voice softened.

"Jesus."

Mildred stroked his thumb with her forefinger.

"At first I couldn't believe it," Elmer said, "but he was looking at me, drawing me into the laughter, even though I fought against it, at first. Then he walked over to me and spoke only once."

"What did he say?" Mildred asked, her hand now resting still on top of her husband's.

"He said, 'where's Mildred?'"

Mildred withdrew her hand from his and slipped it into her pocket.

"Before I could say anything, he took my hand and we began to dance. I couldn't believe it – I felt like a little boy, like when I used to dance with my mother in her kitchen. It's like he reached in, dusted off that memory, and made it new again. There I was dancing with Jesus, and I found myself laughing and singing with him and the others."

Elmer paused a moment, biting down softly on his lower lip. "Then Jesus stopped dancing even though the others continued. Then he looked at me in a different way."

Elmer's words trailed off and a sudden, unfamiliar sadness overcame him.

Mildred patted his hand.

"His eyes changed. I became afraid. I didn't want to look but knew I had to. Can't explain why. I just knew."

"What did they look like – his eyes," Mildred asked.

Elmer's face crinkled into a thinking mode, his thoughts on a quest to honor his wife's question.

"They were burning," he said, "like the last embers of a fire, glowing around the edges but dark in the center – death's eyes. Even though I looked away, his eyes looked into me, through me, into my heart – probin' around into places I had forgotten. Places safe from eyes. But there he was, lookin' – his eyes were like searchlights, seeing everything. I couldn't hide. I tell you, I've never been so ashamed and scared in my life. No matter how tight I held on, those eyes pulled every piece of darkness out of me and set it right down on the front row, then switched on the spotlight. Like the time my father beat me when I was twelve with a leather harness 'cause I had lied to him. He said he was beating the devil out of me, but it hurt so bad that ever since, I felt that anything good had to hurt, that sometimes you had to deny and even hurt the body to save the soul. Like the time I whipped Julie when she was fifteen after I caught her drinking beer with her friends."

Elmer breathed deeply and wiped his brow with his shirt sleeve. Leaning his head back against the old oak tree, he continued. "And there was the time after we were engaged, I sneaked over to Embreeville to see an old girlfriend."

Elmer paused, anticipating a reaction, but was met with only silence.

"I never told you about that and I'm sorry. I'm not that kind of man, and I know you know that. But in that dream, I felt like death had a hold of my belt-loops."

As his words burrowed through her ears, Mildred looked at the fading sun in the distance; her grief hung still in the air like stale laundry on a line.

They both fell silent for awhile. An evening breeze picked up and rustled the leaves above them. The moon traded places with the sun.

Mildred put her hands in her pockets and stood up. The tall grass fell against her ankles.

"Mildred, I looked into his eyes and my heart broke in two."

Tears rolled down Elmer's cheeks as his voice cracked and dropped to a whisper.

"Then his eyes changed again. I was bathed in the look of those eyes . . . like a newborn baby."

The moon blinked in between clouds passing across the sky and Mildred closed her eyes in its light. "Ovenlight," she thought.

She looked at her hands. They were swollen and sore.

Putting her hands back in her pockets, Mildred started off through the tall grass back toward the kitchen door. Elmer turned to look in her direction. He counted silently each step she made.

She stopped and turned to look back at him.

"I'll put some more biscuits in the oven," she said. "Come help me set the table."

10

AS IS

Tommy Wills' dream was always the same, locked away deep, somewhere beneath stacks of faded denim jeans in the attic and an ashtray full of hairpins.

It would begin with a summer Saturday evening. The bathroom window cracked open. The old yellow curtain, the one she never liked, cresting and falling again.

She would let him choose the music, and he'd almost always pull out an old scratched 45 of Gram Parson's "Brass Buttons."

She loved the 'pop' sound when the needle first hit the record. She liked that better than the song itself.

Then she would sit, perched on a stool in front of the old sink, mouthing the words, waiting for him.

Moving toward her, he'd walk as slow as he could, spirits in the old wood floor stirring, alerting them both to each footstep. He always wanted to keep the moment alive for as long as possible.

She would let him pull out her hairpins, one by one, and he'd count each one, laying them gently on the towel shelf. Sometimes he'd pull out the old ukulele that had been hibernating in her mother's attic, the one decorated with jewels from gumball machines. And she would laugh, or roll her eyes, or make up words and sing along.

He would look at her feet while washing her hair and smile at the v-shaped tan lines where she had been wearing flip-flops in the garden.

She would laugh and say, "See it through, Tommy. Stay on course and see it through."

He would dry her off, then wrap her up in an apricot-colored towel, the one with the Corvette Stingray parked in front of a palm tree, the one they got that weekend it rained at the beach.

Then he would lean against the doorway and watch her walk around the hallway corner, to the bedroom. She would always turn and smile just before disappearing, and he'd count each footprint on the floor, left in her wake.

And then she would be gone.

"Wake up sunshine. Break's over. There's a new shipment of Jr. Miss thong sandals with your name on it that's ready to be unloaded and stored in the stockroom."

Tommy lifted his head off his desk and slowly peeled his eyes open, his right hand still wrapped around a Styrofoam coffee cup, wisps of steam drifting from its top.

Ford Fennel, Tommy's 23-year-old assistant manager at the On The Good Foot Shoe Shack, was hovering over him, eyebrows arched and finger tapping against a gold-plated Swiss Army watch.

"Hey listen, I need to cut out a bit early today," he commanded, wiping off his "Get On The Good Foot" sales award pin, which he always wore, even after hours. "Would you mind wrapping up the paperwork, honcho? Got some bidness to tend to."

Tommy took a deep breath, sipped his coffee and glanced over at a small corkboard covered in Polaroid photos of employees. Half of them were of Ford posing with various family automobiles, and more than a few had been "artistically manipulated" by mischievous co-workers wielding Sharpie pens. It was widely known, at least within the confines of The Good Foot, that Ford's parents had named their six children after automobile brand names. Anytime this fact was brought up in conversation among employees, someone would crack, "Which one is Yugo?" or "Is the younger sister named Hyundai, or is that the older sister?" And on and on.

Tommy rubbed his eyes and took a sip of his coffee before standing up.

"Yeah, I can take care of that for you."

"That'd be outstanding."

"Before you leave, though, I'd like to clarify a few things about my history, and perhaps kick a bit of wisdom your way, if you don't mind," Tommy politely asked, sneaking another sip.

Ford, looked at his watch, irritated, and exhaled a deep breath.

"Sure. Shoot."

"For the record, the reason I'm wearing this lovely ankle bracelet here," Tommy said, lifting his khaki pant leg and pointing at the GPS tracking device wrapped around his ankle, "is between me and my parole officer, and it involves neither the rape of someone, nor murder by crowbar."

Ford stood still as a stone, his jaw slack, his eyes frozen wide open. He slowly began reaching for the breakroom door to exit.

"Oh, and Ford . . ."

"Yessir."

"If I ever hear again of you passing off your conspiracy theories as fact concerning why I'm wearing this lovely accessory, I'll find a reason to have a matching one on my other ankle. Clear?"

"As a bell, sir."

Jim "Dandy" James had only been working as a salesman at The Good Foot for four months, but he was already a legend. Dressed immaculate in a suit (even on casual

Fridays), The Dandy would hand pick customers on which to work his self-described "mojitsu" persuasion technique he claimed to have picked up during a dubious tenure in the Orient. He even carried his own personalized Brannock foot measuring device.

In the month of April alone, he convinced 131 customers that orange suede clogs were the harbingers of a nower-than-now Dutch-influenced fashion wave that was still "top seek(ret) in Milan."

The kid was *that* good.

Tommy always tried to guess which color combination The Dandy would assemble for the day's seduction, and this time he was on the money: Khaki linen suit, chocolate & white duotone loafers. He looked sharp as a guillotine and could jaw so well that area car salesmen were known to come in and buy a cheap pair of Adidas just to hijack some of his game.

"Feelin' it today, Tommy boy, rollin' thunder!" The Dandy spoke in a singsong voice, waltzing into the store.

He pulled out a single stick of Juicy Fruit gum from his inside coat pocket, tore it in half, placed one half in his mouth and the unopened piece on the cashier's counter.

"TomTom, visualize with me," he directed from behind the checkout counter, his eyes closed and arms extended out like a tele-evangelist during sweeps week. "Athletic department, third aisle, second shelf. Blonde mother of two. Blue New Balance with Pink trim. Full Retail. A wink and a giggle. Sold, three minutes tops."

The Dandy then shimmied his hands and shot both forefingers toward the more upscale women's shoes selection.

"I see a Steve Madden limited edition boho-stilleto set walking out of here in about five . . . wait," he said, hesitating. "Scratch that. Gimme the Madden bohos, and gimme an additional pair of eggplant-colored aqua socks for the lady at 9 o'clock. By the time the flavor is gone in the gum I'm chewing, it'll be D-U-N, done."

Tommy shook his head and clapped his hands.

"The Dandy do right," he said, smiling. "Make the magic happen, son."

"Yes sir, where you headed?"

"Dinnertime — gonna sample some fine Food Court cuisine and see if I can fatten up this stunning specimen," Tommy answered, patting his generous midsection. "Figured an extra large order of fried won tons will do the trick.'

Tommy grasped the escalator's handrail and began his descent, his fingers tapping in rhythm to the cover version of a cover version of some forgotten song trickling out of the shopping center's speaker system. He looked at the faces of those riding in the opposite direction. Some looked familiar, and most wore what he called "the mall mask" — an expression that's a combination of impatience, anxiety, boredom and frustration.

"Ah, so many choices," Tommy whispered to himself, scanning the Food Court's neon and candy-colored marquees beckoning hungry stomachs. "And so many ways to make your arteries explode."

But he knew which one he'd choose. The same one he always chose (Asian Au Go-Go). At the same time (6:15 p.m., sharp). For the same reason (Celia Skye was the manager, and had provided for the last few weeks, the best dinner companionship he'd had in a long, long time).

Tommy and Celia eased their chairs up to a rare empty table, and that unmistakable Mall Buzz, consisting of pubescent chatter, scattershot laughter, screaming babies and innumerable parental pleas — all wrapped up in a white noise casserole, fell deaf on their ears.

It was just the two of them. . . . and two Moo Goo Gai Pan combo specials, on the house.

Celia tested the heat of the sauce with her index finger and noticed Tommy's tie selection for the day.

"A bolo tie today, huh?," she said, scooping a fork full of food in her mouth. "Looks sharp, Texas Pete."

Tommy smiled, shaking his head.

"My grandfather gave me a collection of these ties when I was a kid. He had a whole wall devoted to 'em. Used to just stand in his room in the summertime, and look at them hanging there, shimmering in the light. Got one for each state. Today is North Dakota's moment in the sun."

"I'm impressed."

"I'm repressed."

Celia laughed out loud, nearly spilling her Coke.

"What is that, a 98 ouncer?" Tommy asked, "They should outfit that thing with a diving board."

"Noooo, it's only a 32 ouncer."

"Oh, *only* a 32 ouncer; that's a sugar O.D. waiting to happen."

Celia smiled and picked at her food a moment.

"Can I ask you something personal?" she asked.

"Shoot."

"For weeks, we've been gathering at this table together, you and I, and I'm looking at that wedding ring on your finger. And I take it that, from the direction our conversation has been flowing here, you're not married — am I right?"

"Mmhm. That's true."

"So, may I ask why you still wear the ring?"

Tommy pulled his straw out of his cup lid and poked at the lukewarm remnants of his Moo Goo Gai Pan. The dinner rush was beginning to fade a bit.

"My wife passed away five years ago next week. Cancer."

Celia shook her head, tucking her hair behind her ears.

"I'm so sorry."

Tommy carefully pushed his plate aside and held up his left hand

"She made this ring for me. She was an artisan — stained glass, pottery. A real hands-on type," Tommy continued, putting the straw back in his cup. "After she passed, I went out of my mind, pretty much. The usual

TV Movie Of The Week-type stuff. Heavy drinking, lost the big job, lost the house. Lost it all. Thank God we didn't have kids."

Celia crumpled her napkin and placed it on her near-empty plate of food as Tommy continued.

"So one night, after celebrating my grief — *yet again* — I drove my 1987 Mercury Cougar into the broadside of a parked car. Two young ladies were inside, gussied up for an evening out. The impact of my car killed the girl in the passenger side. Michelle Dubois. 20 years old. Economics major at Georgia Tech. On the verge of everything.

"Such a beautiful girl," his voice trailed off. "A real beaut."

"I was sentenced to five years in prison. Michelle's family, understandably, wanted my throat slit in front of the television cameras. My friends turned into ghosts . . . but I did the time, and here I am — an ex-convict salesman, fourth best in the bunch, for The Good Foot, with a boss half my age . . . and this lovely little fashion accessory.

Tommy lifted his left pant leg to reveal a black, belt-like strap just above his ankle.

"It's a GPS tracking device, a Global Positioning Satellite tracks my every move and reports to my probation officer," he said. "Very James Bond, huh?"

Celia wiped her hands on her napkin and reached to graze the strap with her finger.

"Is it heavy?"

"Was at first, but you get used to it. Thought I might debut it at the beach this summer, start a new fashion trend."

"I'd love to see that," Celia answered, laughing. "Next stop: the runways of Par-eeee!"

Tommy and Cecilia both laughed out loud, the Food Court's buzz now a post-dinner rush hum.

"So, anyway, the only connection to her I had left was this ring, which the boys in blue slipped into a little Ziplock bag for safekeeping while I was in prison. And when I was released, it was the first thing I saw that reminded me of the life I had outside — of life with her. It's all I have left."

Celia leaned in toward Tommy and tucked her hair behind both ears.

"I think you have a little more left than you realize," she said.

A faint smile cracked across Tommy's face. He reached to pull his pant leg down over the strap strangling his ankle.

"No, don't," Celia said, waving his hand away from his pant leg. "Leave it as is."

Tommy paused for a moment and looked at Celia. He thought about her voice. It was warm and cozy as a lap.

Celia took a long sip of coffee, and Tommy watched a wisp of steam rise from its lid, smeared with lipstick.

She unfolded one of the crumpled napkins on her dinner plate, pulled out a pen and began writing.

"Do you think about her often," she asked, still writing.

"She's always there," he said, "kind of like a loose shoe string that keeps clicking against the floor when you walk."

Celia folded the napkin neatly, removed a hairpin from her tangle of brown curls, and clipped the napkin onto Tommy's bolo tie.

"You been walking in those shoes a long time, Tommy," she said, standing up. "Maybe it's about time for a new pair."

Tommy unfolded the napkin.

It read: "Wanted: Tall ex-convict. Brown eyes, bald. Bad taste in ties. Will take him as is. If interested, call Celia at 770.881.3224."

After carefully folding the napkin and slipping it in his shirt pocket, Tommy held Celia's hairpin up to the light and smiled.

"770.881.3224," he repeated to himself, over and over, humming the numbers as if they were words in the melody of a song he thought he had forgotten to sing.

11

TRUTH TELLER

Two years ago I saw the truth.

Two years and fifteen minutes ago I started speaking it.

My life hasn't been worth a damn since.

I always heard that the truth will make you free.

Free from what? I'll tell you what. In the span of two short years, I was freed from my career, my wife and daughter, and even from the lousy efficiency apartment I have been living in for the last two months.

Hell yes, I'm free.

Free to take my last three hundred bucks and hit the open road in a worn-out Ford Taurus, 160,000 miles young. Free from everything that made my life what it was — everything that I wanted and worked for.

Two short years ago on a cold Friday evening I was nursing my third Sam Adams and bullshitting with the regular   end-of-the-week-upper-management-wannabees for the *City Daily News.*

I was at the top of the mid-level career food chain where I toiled for my living. A Master of Arts degree in journalism and ten years of busting my ass had brought me to the edge of greatness and to Buddy's Bar on what turned out to be a cold day in hell.

As a hard-working assistant editor in charge of the sports and features sections, I was just a skip and jump and some well-placed ass kissing away from one of the two prized associate executive editors' slots. Given the inevitability of Ed McMann's impending retirement, that soon-to-be-vacant office with its own bathroom and big picture window had my name written all over it.

I had another advantage over the beer and bourbon swizzling reprobates I drank with during our Friday evening rituals. They had their eye on the same elusive prize that I did, but unlike them, I could actually write. Yeah, I was kicking ass and kissing ass — a lethal combination that pointed like a champion bird dog sitting on a covey of quail to the golden ring I was about to grab. A ring that would make me and mine proud and the envy of all the other yahoos at the *City Daily News.*

Trouble is, I drank one beer too many because it was during that third beer that fate stepped in and punctured my balloon of ambition, laying waste to life as I knew it.

During that third beer I overheard Geraldine Stevens talking to the bartender about her sorry-ass husband. Several black eyes, a neck brace, and her son's increased bed wetting had lit a fire under her that only fear and loneliness kept in check. Enough was enough. Geraldine was ready to leave the worthless son-of-a-bitch she was married to and return to her parents in South Alabama. Trouble was, she was broke. As soon as she could put her hands on enough cash for two bus tickets, she and her son were heading south to freedom. At least that's what she told the bored bartender who was practicing the time-worn bartender's art of pretending to give a damn.

That's what she was telling him. But I knew better. The king-size gimlet she was sucking on was doing the talking for her and her boy. My guess was that she was at least a broken arm or preteen suicide attempt away from speaking for herself and acting like the mother she was pretending to be.

Yeah, I could see right through her. It was like I had known her all my life. And I didn't like what I saw. So be it. A quick trip to the men's room to relieve myself and I would be on my way home to Natalie and Natasha, my wife and daughter, respectively.

I even remember the sound of zipping up my Dockers and feeling the cold blast of air that hit me in the face as I stepped out to hail a cab on that armpit of a February night.

As I waved my arms to no avail, none other than Geraldine, the gimlet swizzler, exited the bar and sidled up next to me.

She stood too close for comfort and I didn't like the way she looked at me. It was like she wanted something. I stamped my feet against the cold and she just stood there looking at me as if she wanted to speak but was waiting for permission. I was thinking that sometimes strangers are best left strangers when she spoke.

Unlike the I'll-tell-you-a-thing-or-two voice from inside the bar, she asked me in a child's uncertain whisper, "Will you help me get a cab?"

That's what she said, but what I heard through some strange cosmic filter of fate was, "Will you HELP ME?"

Not taking my eyes off her, I stepped back in shock and *spoke*. I never do that — speak what I see.

The conversations of truth as I see it, should stay where they belong — in one's head. But not this time. This time it spoke me.

Offering her the contents of my wallet, I said,"Geraldine, you need to leave that worthless bastard and go home to your parents before you lose yourself or worse — your son's life."

Geraldine's jaw dropped and she looked as if she were about to reply. Instead, she snatched the money out of my hand and hopped into the cab that had just pulled up as if on cue in some third-rate movie.

That's right. She took the money and got into the cab without so much as a thank you. Did she go home, retrieve her son, and take the next bus to Alabama?

Damned if I know.

All I recall is that for the first time I could remember, I spoke what I saw.

Holding my empty wallet, I walked home in the cold to the waiting warmth of Natalie's inquisition.

Although I stayed away from Buddy's Bar, it didn't seem to help calm my new-found affliction. The truth had me by the balls and every time it squeezed, I spoke. I wanted to keep my thoughts to myself, but possessed by a clarity of insight I never imagined and an inability to remain silent, I could feel myself sinking ever deeper into the quicksand of opportunity.

Two months after my encounter with Geraldine, I elicited the same dumbfounded look of incredulity from my boss, Ned Jasper who — rumor had it — was about to appoint me associate editor.

The words rushed out, dragging my reluctant voice with them.

"Ned, we've been friends a long time, but I've got to tell you, screwing that journalism intern isn't worth your twenty-year marriage to Marge, not to mention the respect of your children."

Ned's response was to the point.

"Get out!"

As it turned out, his retort foretold a wider arc of response than I ever would have anticipated.

"Get out" not only referred to the immediacy of that embarrassing moment in his office, but also came to include the newspaper itself. Needless to say, I didn't get the promotion and soon-after found myself reassigned to the "eastern front" of newspaper work — reporting on city commission and board meetings.

The day I finally resigned I tried to explain to Natalie that personal integrity was more important than a promotion or a particular kind of job. Her expression of disapproval fed the hidden part of me that agreed with her.

Six months and a series of unsuccessful interviews and substitute teaching assignments later, Natalie uttered what has become a refrain in my life. Between sips of orange juice, Natalie's mouth opened and Ned Jasper's voice seemed to speak through her early morning smoker's rasp.

"Get out!"

So I did.

I left it all behind, not willingly, but of necessity.

Even Natasha shed no visible tears the day I left with suitcase in hand. The last sound I heard was a good riddance bark from Bobo, the cocker spaniel.

In short order, I went from writing for the newspaper to delivering newspapers. My pre-dawn route combined with education's constant need for inner city substitute teachers, afforded me the luxury of a well-worn efficiency on 10th Avenue and evening forays to Buddy's, where Mike, the bartender, offered me the same courtesy he had given to Geraldine a year earlier.

My friend, Sam Adams, was too rich for my current financial fortunes so I mingled with his more budget-minded kin and attempted to sort out what had become of my existence. I surmised to Mike that at least I was reasonably confident that things couldn't get any worse.

I was wrong.

I struck up an ill-fated friendship with my landlord, Buck LePew. Buck apparently saw some semblance of the management potential in me that Ned and my former wife had given up on. In exchange for managing the eight-unit apartment house I resided in, I got to live rent-free.

A spark of my former self slowly began to re-emerge as I considered my future prospects in the field of residential management. As I became more familiar with Buck's enterprise, I soon realized that some rocks were best not overturned. A clear pattern emerged of compounding the misery of elderly tenants on fixed incomes by excessively raising their rent and ignoring their pleas for repairs and basic service. Forcing such undesirables out of their apartments allowed the vacated units to be rented to higher paying young professionals.

Even as I tried to maintain control, I could feel that ugly entity known as a conscience beginning to awaken and take shape. It wouldn't be long before my tongue would begin to work its black magic.

I still remember the day Buck LePew, chewing nervously on a cigar stub, was held captive by the logic of truth's outpouring.

I had just finished an impressive oration that concluded by telling Buck that he was too good of a person to torture his elderly residents for nothing more than a little extra filthy lucre, not to mention that what he did to them, good or bad, would be returned to him ten-fold.

Buck LePew said two things in response to my well-intentioned query.

His first response was, "Who the hell do you think you are, some crazy-ass prophet?

Then he uttered those dreaded, oft-told words.

"Get Out!"

I still remember the last moments I spent at Buck's establishment. My bag was packed and positioned next to the door, and I stood in the bathroom, looking out the window. I was lost in my thoughts. Not just in my thoughts, it was me that was lost. I had nowhere to go. I had nothing. I was nothing.

I peered out the frost-encrusted window and all I could see was a barren bush with a single branch reaching toward me. On the end of it was a single bud.

My wet face pressed against the glass.

It was a beautiful thing.

12

BALLAD OF THE WAFFLEHOUSE QUEEN

With a smile as thin as a crack in a church pew, Neevis Starly looked out the frost-dusted window of the Highway 73 Wafflehouse and noticed a sad, single strand of dollar store Christmas lights strung along the rusted tailgate of a Ford pickup. The letters "F-O-R-D" had been replaced with "L-O-R-D", and the bulbs, doing their best to institute an air of holiday enchantment, flickered like pale stars against the grey swell of Kentucky winter.

Neevis slipped on a gold-striped cardigan, the initials "NS" embroidered above the left breast pocket, and turned her attention to Heston Golly, a store fixture seated on the counter corner, his traditional hash brown special pushed aside to make way for three different newspapers, each edition set out in front of him in near-perfect symmetry. An older man of hefty build,

Heston was dressed in his customary garb (head-to-toe in blue denim jacket, vest & jeans; a khaki ascot; and silver-tipped cowboy boots). Nestled against his coffee cup on the countertop was a blue and white baseball cap that read in large square letters, "MUCHACHO." Scattershot flecks of fried egg decorated his long twist of pepper gray beard like ornaments on a tree.

"Heston," she tossed in his direction, her thin lips pulling back like a theater curtain, revealing a silver-toothed smile. "This is the kind of cold that would make you shoot somebody just to feel the warmth of the barrel."

The old man squinted, looked up at her over the rim of his glasses and shook his head – filing the comment away in the stacks of "Neevis-isms" scattered all over his memory – and reached for his coffee cup.

"Just give me a head-start before you pull the trigger," he answered in between quick sips, turning his attention back to his newspapers.

A closer look at Heston's prized corner stool revealed a gold-plated "Preferred Clientele" etching, located on the back of the seat's chrome strip plating. The corner-counter seat had been his perch for nearly three decades, including a 10-year absence during which, out of respect, no one had dared slip atop his throne, not even for a cup of coffee.

For decades, shambling Store 73 had offered budget-friendly solace for bleary eyed travelers snaking their way through the two-lane tangles of southeast Kentucky by-ways, and Neevis, known to a host of locals as "the biscuit baroness," was as much a part of its late-night lineage as the bricks and mortar. For nearly 40 years, her tireless, muscled hips had served her well, her brisk deliveries ushering all manner of eats from grill to table with the kind of "honey baby" panache only a seasoned pro could will or muster (a gift that earned her "Tip-Top Titleist" 9 years running – an unparalleled display of patron-pleasing prowess – beginning in the early 1970's). To commemorate her feat, former manager Tavis Pickles even named a "seasonal special" in her honor – "the Starly Spangled Sundae" (a number-one seller during summer of 1980).

But just as the days tumble and disappear into time's ever-turning cosmic till, Neevis' once golden hips had now downshifted into an autumnal gear, needing frequent rest stops. To accommodate and ease the impact of such physical ravages, she began placing three chairs behind the service bar – each claimed by a different name: Betty (cash register), Billy Boy (drink prep) and Burly Bob (grill), the sturdiest of the three.

The "Boys," as she called them, always helped ease the stress and strain of the late shift and helped negotiate a comfortable transition to the morning's more manageable coffee & paper crowd.

With a pin-point precision and surgical focus that would make Neevis proud, eight-year-old LuLu Chimera poured pools of Winchester Rye maple syrup (the house blend)

into each crisp divot of her waffle, which had been chewed around the edges until it vaguely resembled the letter "L." A thicket of curls, auburn and unruly, sprouted from her tiny scalp like coil springs, and her full cheeks served as an improvised canvas for assorted finger-painted inspirations – a sunflower one day, a lightning bolt the next.

Between 4 a.m. and noon each weekend, Table 3 belonged to LuLu; it was a loosely regulated residence, serving as nursery, playground and confessional – all in one. And she rarely left its pleather purgatory – unless Neevis gave her permission – or her father, a late shift dishwasher, punched his timecard and signaled for a swift and often wordless exit from the premises.

Neevis lined up six coffee filters on the prep counter in anticipation of the breakfast rush and peeked over the counter at LuLu's table to check in on the artist in residence.

"Easy on the syrup, mi pajarito, bonita; there won't be anything left for paying customers."

LuLu, her large sleepy eyes a congregation of colors dominated by caramel and hazel, looked up and smiled at Neevis, the sight of that silver tooth always sparking sensations of delight and comfort. As was tradition when Neevis slipped in a Spanish phrase or two in conversation, LuLu reached for the well-thumbed-through English-to-Spanish dictionary that stayed sandwiched atop her table between a stack of comment cards and twin salt & pepper shakers. Every morning she found the book in the same place, and each time, there mysteriously appeared new bacon grease-stained notes and comments scribbled in the margins.

"*Mi pajarito bonita*," she whispered to herself flipping through the pages.

Neevis smiled, dipped her left forefinger into a yellow dab of LuLu's finger-paints, and delicately smudged the little girl's cheek.

"There, we need a little spot of sunshine on mornings like this, don't we?" she said, sliding a cleaning cloth from her right shoulder and, with patented efficiency and flair, cracking it like a bullwhip in Heston's direction.

He just shook his head without offering a verbal response, a coffee cup firmly planted to his lips.

LuLu turned to look out the window into the winter gray skies; someone had etched "a band aid for the hartbreak kid" into the window frost, and scraped a heart shape around it.

"They spelled 'heartbreak' wrong," she thought to herself.

LuLu's tiny feet, interlocked and clad in pink clogs, dangled above the floor and swung side to side to the loping rhythm of "Sleepwalk," by crooner Santo & Johnny (Neevis claimed the outfit's drummer once stopped by the store one foggy night years ago to use the bathroom and accidentally locked himself in a stall. County Sheriff's deputy Raines Randis was notified of the incident, arrived on the scene as discreetly as possible and made a diligent effort to free the musician, only to end up locking himself in the very same stall). That was the rumor, anyway.

A small, tattered piñata, constructed poorly to re-semble what was supposed to be a winged horse hung high and aloft in a precarious state of suspension near the overhead air vent, faint gusts of conditioned air pro-pelling its perilous flight. The ramshackle creation was the mascot for the Keeneland Fraternal Order Of The Pegasus, whose members held a "breakfast summit" the first Saturday of each month. Though Neevis didn't ap-prove of the unsightly symbol's presence in the store, the group never failed to tip generously, and in her book, that was good enough.

LuLu noticed sun-faded stripes of color in the craft-ed creature's wings and decided to emulate its guise with an interpretation of her own. She sopped her fingertips in the splotches of paint that had now spilled out of her dime store purse and onto her placemat, and traced three stripes – blue, red, yellow – on each of her cheeks. Startled by the muted thump of the washroom door swinging open, LuLu turned to see a man emerge, his apron stained by a panorama of morning demands, washroom scars and oth-er traces of minimum wage humility. He moved through the restaurant with brisk purpose, his stride unbroken, and his line of vision locked on the floor. Wafting past LuLu like a ghost, he emptied himself out the front door without uttering a word.

As if snapped by an imaginary leash tethered to the man's belt, Lulu dropped her finger paints and slipped out of her booth in one swift motion, stumbling and los-ing her left shoe in the process. She caught the door with her tiny hands just before it closed, and felt the piercing uppercut of winter's rude salutation.

After a brief scouting mission, she found the man leaning against the restaurant's back-end loading dock, ashes growing from a cigarette wedged between his fingers, clouds circling the sky above his head like phantoms.

Her thin bones shivering, LuLu watched thick funnels of cigarette smoke, illuminated by the parking lot's pale lamplight, billow from the man's nostrils – like the bull caricature painted on the window of Mertin's Five An' Dime downtown.

"*Toro*," she whispered to herself, her cautious steps carrying her to the edge of the man's long shadow.

"What?" he let out in a delivery that was switchblade short.

"Toro," she repeated, padding forward and tucking her hair behind her right ear. "It means "bull" in Spanish – *Española*. I learned that from Neevis. She teaches me a new word everyday."

The man shook his head and took a long drag from his cigarette as LuLu moved another step closer.

"Daddy, I–"

"Don't call me that," he interrupted, his words cutting so quick and clean they left no blood behind.

She stood small and crooked in his shadow, her ears ringing, muting out the sounds of passing traffic in the distance.

He moved toward her and leaned in closer, his eyes all hard glass and hidden. In them, she could see her own reflection – warped and shapeless.

The man rubbed his scalp, toed an invisible line between himself and LuLu's feet, and turned away, pulling the last moments of life from his cigarette – the funnels from his nostrils continuing to billow, thick and ceaseless.

Eyes shut tight, he leaned back against the brick wall and looked up at the moon, its visage still obscured by a veil of clouds.

"Neevis will take you home tonight," he said, flicking a spark of ash onto the pavement. "Now hop back in the store and let me finish up my business here."

Looking through a thin steam curtain rising from his coffee cup, Heston Golly took a deep sip and watched Lulu shuffle back in from the cold and slip her tiny frame into the far-side booth of Table 3. She paused for a moment, doll-still and vacant eyed. Only her fingers were animated, twitching like out-of-tune keys on a player piano. The moment passed quickly, though, and she was back at work giving another freshly sculpted "L"-shaped waffle a syrupy baptism.

Heston tapped the countertop with his ring finger, just as he always did after finishing a meal, slipped on his cap and took one last sip of coffee before digging into his front pocket for his money clip.

LuLu lifted her head to catch a glimpse of the old man's slow waddle toward the cash register. She liked the clip-clop sound of his cowboy boots as he walked. Holding up her forefinger, she closed one eye and made a quiet click sound with her tongue, taking an imaginary snapshot of Heston. She repeated his cap moniker, "*Muchacho*," to herself in a whisper, and stretched to retrieve her trusty paperback translator to determine the word's origin.

"You'll have to pardon the hitch in my giddy-up, young 'un," Heston said, a quiet triplet of deep laughs escaping his throat. "That's what happens when you become a permanent resident of Old-Man's-Ville. You get to stumbling, bumbling and tumbling."

Heston paused for a moment, slipped his denim-covered money clip back into his pocket, and slid his aching frame into the booth on the other side of LuLu's table.

"You changing the face of the art world over here?" he asked, smiling and surveying her early morning creations. "They should call you the Wafflehouse Picasso."

LuLu smiled, put down her dictionary, and focused her concentration on Heston's thick knuckles. She leaned toward them and read aloud the faded blue numbers tattooed along their calloused ridges. "My daddy got numbers like that on his, too," she said.

Heston stretched his back and offered a faint smile.

"I figured he might be acquainted with such decorative accouterments," he added, reaching for the packet of Chesterfield Kings he kept in his coat pocket – before remembering Neevis' authoritative "no smoking" policy, which hanged eye-level next to hat rack: "*We don't serve Black Lung here. Sorry. – Management.*"

Without hesitation, LuLu began placing dabs of color on Heston's arthritic knuckles, each one awarded a different shade and hue.

"Daddy always keeps his hands in his pockets when we're around people so they don't see his marks," she said, still applying her color combinations with great care and concentration. "You know my daddy?"

"Well, we've never had an opportunity to exchange pleasantries," the old man answered, "but sometimes you can know what a person's bones are made of without sharing so much as a handshake."

"What are my bones made of?" LuLu asked, her eyes acutely reviewing her first-ever "knuckle art" installation, thanks to Heston's cooperative amusement.

"Something stronger than what I carry in mine, I'd most certainly speculate," he answered, his flint-gray eyes noticing scattered bruises of varying shapes and sizes decorating her thin bare arms. She had made attempts to cover them up with self-rendered finger-paintings of sunshine, flowers and butterflies, but these were sights not unfamiliar to Heston. Long ago, he had – at different times in his life – both endured and inflicted similar handiwork. And in the bent and barb-wired days of his youth, he spent 10-years incarcerated for being unable to holster his angry hands.

Breathing deeply, Heston bowed his head and shut his eyes for a moment to, as he always put it, "let the ghost pass through the door notch."

He reached into the left breast pocket of his denim jacket and retrieved a frayed box of crayons, the corners torn and taped (and re-taped) back together. Some of the colors were missing, others were broken. A root beer scratch & sniff sticker shaped like the letter "A" decorated the back of the box.

He placed the box in front of LuLu.

"Think you can make some magic with these?" he asked.

"Who does the 'A' stand for?" she inquired, investigating the box as a jeweler might appraise the value of a stone.

"Stands for someone who was about your age; someone who was very special to me."

"What happened to her?"

"Well. I lost her to the Lord," Heston said after a slim moment of hesitation, cracks forming in his voice. "He surmised – and rightfully so – that I wasn't fit to take care of her at that time in my life."

LuLu nudged the old weathered pack back in his direction, across the table.

"Well maybe the Lord will give her back to you someday."

Heston smiled and tapped his ring finger against the table.

"I kind of feel like he already has. Tell you what – why don't you hold on to these for me. I been carrying them around a long time, and sometimes things get real heavy if you carry 'em around long enough. Besides, I think I found the right person to make good use of them, don't you?"

Lulu smiled and shrugged.

"I want to show you something," he said, rolling up his sleeves. "See these, here?"

He pulled back both sleeves revealing two identical tattoos – one on each of his forearms. They were shaped like chrome bird's wings, angular and detailed, as if cut from the grill of a vintage automobile. Each wing hosted an illustrated hinge, "bolted" to his arms.

Lulu reached to trace them with her fingers, her eyes full of electricity, having never seen such elaborate artistry.

"When I was about your Daddy's age, a long time ago, I got involved with some bad people, Heston said softly, leaning in closer, "and sometimes, when you get involved with bad people, you're liable to do some bad things. Well I done some things I'm not proud of, and for a long time, I thought I was trapped, that it was over-and-out – 'the endsville' – stuff like that. But an old man – a friend of mine – told me I had a way out. Said I had secret wings inside me, and they would take me anywhere I wanted to go, if I believed in them."

Heston reached over and dipped his forefinger and middle finger into LuLu's blue paint palette and gently traced out the shape of bird wings on her tiny forearms.

"Now, I know I don't have your painterly eye," he said, a hollow cough ushered out with his words, "but these to me carry the appearance of some pretty good lookin' bluebird wings. Nah, scratch that – we'll call 'em *LuBird* wings. What do you think about that?"

LuLu laughed out loud, her delight refusing to stay at room temperature.

"You ready to take flight?"

"Yessir."

"Well, I'm gonna pay Miss Neevis for that dee-lish breakfast, skippity-doo-da out of here, and bid your lovely self adieu. I want you to take what's in that Crayon box and pretty up the world a bit, 'kay?"

"It's hard for me to keep it inside the lines," LuLu replied. "I'm not real good at that."

Heston shuffled back toward her, pulled his hat brim tight over his forehead, and bent down, placing his hands on his knees.

"Listen here: There ain't many things in this life worth a *damn* that's drawn in a straight line. Put your arms around the crooked things in this world and hold 'em tight, okay? Promise me?"

"I promise."

Heston dropped three crisp bills clipped to a note for Neevis on the counter and walked toward the door, stopping a moment to tap his ring finger on the door handle and turn to LuLu.

"Keep those wings spread, LuBird. As wide as you can – always."

LuLu watched the old man waddle out into the morning fog. She turned to look at the tattered, winged horse, hanging from the ceiling corner, its stray strands of color slowly growing more vibrant with the coming dawn light. Eyes wide open, she looked at her painted forearms and imagined herself piloting a papery-winged steed high over milky winter skies and other worldly darkness – hurtling together toward a kingdom in the sun.

13

AMNESIA OF THE HEART

"All these fru-fru snacks—sesame sticks, snow peas and pine nuts. How about some old-fashioned, all-American snacks? Have they passed a law against serving plain old salted peanuts?" Jack Hamilton said more to himself than anyone else as he sat nursing his second bourbon and water at the bar in the Holiday Inn just off the I-85 exit near Greenville.

The green, silk floor plants and artfully placed strands of white Christmas lights framed the "Generations" Bistro and Bar. The bartender positioned herself as far away as possible from Jack Hamilton, pretending to dry wine glasses that were already dry. She had seen his kind before—retired, lonely men who felt entitled to rerun their Nick-at-Night life stories for the price of several bourbons. The Christmas season brought them out in full force. Separated from her husband after one year of marriage and facing a psychology final in the morning was enough stress for Sylvia. She would keep him supplied with bourbon and "fru-fru" snacks as he put it, but nothing else.

A cold rush of December burst into the tiny bar as a middle-aged, heavy-set man made his way to the counter and removed his parka.

"How 'bout a Bud Lite, Ma'am?"

"Coming right up," Sylvia replied as she reached into the cooler. "You want some party mix?"

"Yeah, sure. Why not?"

The sound of dulcimer inspired Christmas music wafted into the bar from the restaurant. Jack turned toward the stranger. "How's the traffic?"

"Busy."

The two men drank in silence, serenaded by dulcimers and the sounds of interstate traffic as Sylvia hid behind a newspaper.

Jack turned again to the stranger.

"Let me buy you a drink."

"Sure, why not," the man answered, extending his hand in appreciation. "Thanks."

"How bout a Bud Lite for my friend and another Jimmy Beam and water for me, Missy?"

"Coming right up. Would you like some more 'fru-fru'— I mean party mix?" Sylvia offered, her face turning slightly crimson.

Jack's brow crinkled slightly in amusement. "Yeah. And you had it right the first time. Give us another helping of 'fru-fru'."

The two men tipped their glasses to each other and continued drinking while Sylvia placed their glasses in the dishwasher, grateful that the new customer had taken the pressure off her for conversation. From dulcimers to Zamfir's pan flute, the Christmas music continued to make its way from the restaurant in muted and muffled tones.

"Where you headed?" Jack inquired as he searched his dish for an elusive peanut.

"I'm going south for Christmas. Down to 'Hotlanta.' How about you?"

"Guess I'll stay around here. Got a condo not too far from here."

The stranger seemed to be warming up to his libation benefactor much to the relief of Sylvia.

"Don't much like to be alone at Christmas. Going to my brother's and his family. Me and my wife split up last year. Been married ten years when she up and ran off with the plumber. Always thought jokes about wives and plumbers were pretty funny 'til my wife ran off with one."

"Sorry to hear about that," Jack replied, taking a long pull from his bourbon and water.

"Yeah, me too. Whole thing caught me by surprise. My job took me on the road a lot. Every time I came home, there'd be another plumbing problem that needed fixin'. Never suspected a thing. The house was two years old. That's what we always worked toward—to have a new house of our own. That's what I wanted—a new house. I got the house and the plumber got my wife. Guess I got the best damn plumbing in my neighborhood. How stupid is that?"

Jack lit a cigarette. "We all got plenty of stupid in us. Here I am sitting in a bar, drinking and eating 'fru-fru' party mix two days before Christmas while my daughter wonders why I won't spend Christmas with her, my two grand-daughters, Susie and Edie, and her husband, Ed."

"Ed must be a jerk."

"No, Ed's okay. He's been a good husband and provider. I couldn't ask for a better son-in-law."

"I don't get it," the stranger said, reaching for the party mix. "What about your wife? Maybe she and Ed don't get along too well. Hope he's not a plumber."

Jack chuckled softly. "No Ed's no plumber. He's in insurance. Fact is, my wife died six years ago of cancer."

Jack's drinking companion stopped eating.

"Sorry to hear that."

"That's alright. It was hard to lose her, but when you see someone suffer like she did. . . ."

Jack looked away and cleared his throat.

Returning to his drink, he looked at Sylvia, still hiding behind the newspaper.

"Missy, how bout another round for me and . . . ."

"Name's Tom McElroy," the stranger interrupted, extending his hand. "I'll buy the next round."

"Well, thank you kindly, Tom," Jack replied, extending his own. "I'm Jack Hamilton."

The drinks arrived with more party mix.

"Don't mean to pry Jack, but for the life of me, I can't figure out why you're not with your daughter and her family eating turkey and dressing instead of drinking Jim Beam and eating party mix with me. I mean, I wish I had a daughter like that. Me and my wife never had kids. I love my brother and his family, but being an Uncle ain't like being a Daddy."

"You got a point Tom. It's my own fault. Strange as it sounds, I just don't feel that comfortable at my daughter's."

With the confidence that three Bud Lite's can bring, Tom pressed Jack a bit.

"Why don't you feel comfortable? Sounds pretty comfortable to me."

Jack took another swallow of his bourbon.

"Truth is, I don't know my daughter all that well. I retired from the FBI ten years ago. My wife pretty much raised her. I put my work first. Thought I was doing it for my family, but that was only partly true. I was as married to the Bureau as I was to Jill and Hope."

Jack swirled his drink with a swizzle stick and continued.

"Hope was a beautiful baby. I remember when I brought her and her mother home from the hospital. What a day it was. I remember Jill and me taking her to her first day of school. Got to attend one or two dance recitals, but missed most of them due to work. I was on assignment in D.C. when she went to her first prom, but the pictures turned out great. Likewise, her high school graduation. Me and Jill did make it to her college graduation, but work kept me from a lot of the stuff in between. Then she and Ed got married.

She was some beautiful bride. I cried like a baby when I gave her away. I was glad none of my bureau buddies saw me . . . none of them could make the wedding. Then she and Ed had Susie and little Edie."

Jack looked away again and rubbed his left eye as Tom looked down at the party mix dish.

"Every year since Jill died, Hope asks me to come up for Thanksgiving and stay through Christmas. And every year, I promise to do it . . . and I mean to. After a few days I always end up leaving and coming home. I start feeling out-of-place a day or two after Thanksgiving. I love my daughter, but in a way, I don't know her. I've got some good memories, but in between those memories are gaps—a lifetime of empty spaces. She and Ed still invite me each year, but I can hear it in their voices. They know I won't stay. I feel guilty about the whole thing. I made my bed and I guess I'll have to lie in it."

Jack grew silent, lost in his spent opportunities. Even Sylvia, peeking from behind her newspaper found herself drawn into Jack's predicament. Tom said nothing as he chewed on a toothpick and stared at a snow pea laying on the counter.

Taking the toothpick from his mouth, Tom looked at his newfound acquaintance.

"Jack, you know a person can change beds. My wife sure did. She didn't give me a chance to make up the gaps— or if she did, I was too dumb to notice. Can't do nothing 'bout the gaps of the past, but you also got some good memories to build on. Ain't like your daughter's holding those gaps against you. I know it ain't easy, but none of us got forever to make things right. And maybe you can't even if you try. Question is, are you running from your chances or toward 'em?"

Jack felt his neck stiffen up. He didn't particularly like what he heard, but if thirty years at the Bureau taught him one thing, it was to listen—to pay attention before he reacted.

"You got a point, Tom, but it's two days before Christmas. They wouldn't be expecting me. They probably have other plans."

Jack chuckled, "They'd probably have a heart attack if I showed up on their doorstep Christmas Eve."

"Maybe that's the kind of heart attack they're wishing for this Christmas," Tom replied, smiling as he got up from the bar and placed a five-dollar tip on the counter. "I got to be getting on to 'Hotlanta.' My folks'll be expecting me."

"I need to get going too," Jack responded, rising from his stool. "Merry Christmas, Missy."

"Merry Christmas, fellows. You both drive safe now," Missy replied as she scooped the tip money into her apron.

The two men shook hands outside the bar and wished each other a happy holiday.

"Tom, if you ever get this way again, look me up. I'm in the phone book."

"I might just take you up on that," Tom replied. "You gonna call her?"

Jack looked at Tom and smiled. "Don't know. Maybe."

With a wave of his hand, Tom was gone. Jack watched his tail lights disappear into the cold, December night. It was beginning to snow as Jack zipped his parka all the way up to his chin.

Climbing into his Ford pick-up, Jack lit a cigarette and looked at the cell phone lying on the seat next to him. He cranked up the truck and exhaling a plume of smoke, whispered, "Reach out and touch someone."

14

STRAY DOGS

With a grace and sureness of step that belied her considerable size, Minnie Cook briskly climbed the Cook's Dimestore Dream stock-ladder, stretched one desperate arm above a stockpile of tin Raggedy Andy lunchboxes and flicked at the store radio's volume dial, transforming Bing Crosby's swelling croon to a hush. The Dream's old wood floorboards creaked as she backed her heft down each rung, and three wood bracelets — green, red, green — on her left arm click-clacked with each brisk movement.

Heights made Minnie nervous, and her role was usually relegated to operating and protecting the store's cash register, but on this day in which a brick suddenly found itself lodged — dead center — in the store's primary display window, emergency maneuvers were warranted.

The nervous corner of Minnie's mouth twitched as she peered above the origami reindeer mounted atop the cash register and watched her husband, Simpsey, standing eyes closed and motionless inside the storefront's display window, which was now a cracked pane of glass on the verge of collapse.

Simpsey could feel the warmth of the setting December sun on his face, and a soft breeze found its way through the window's cracks, which fanned out like a spider web from the brick's impact point. He slowly opened his eyes and made a soft-boned attempt to calm the escalating anger rising from his boots. The breeze continued to blow through the hole, past the brick, past Simpsey, through the aisles of Cook's Dimestore Dream, dislodging a stack of cheap plastic Halloween masks that had been sleeping beneath a blanket of dust in the bargain bin for months. The crisp December burst sent them skittering, a half-dozen or so Donnie & Marie Osmond faces, across the floor.

Bing's voice on the radio was barely a hush now, interrupted by the periodic tinkle of glass shards falling to the floor.

Simpsey reached out with his left hand to graze the tip of the brick, its jagged point an angry finger jutting back at him. His right hand, growing blood red, grasped the blunt wood hull of a brushless broom handle, which he kept as a constant companion to help defend his struggling business from what he considered to be "the stray dog scourge." Etched on the stick's chipped wood shaft were the words The Educator, and as an unfortunate handful of bruised and knotted young men could testify to, The Educator bore hard, painful lessons. Hijacking a fistful of Chick 'O Sticks could cost you a broken finger or two. A failed attempt to swipe a soda from the Tastee-Pop cooler would be heartily rewarded with swift strokes to the back, the groin, the head. Didn't matter. Simpsey wielded The Educator like a butcher worked a meat cleave. And for any off-colored comments directed at Simpsey's wife, Minnie?

Few, if any, had even hatched the thought.

Still motionless, Simpsey caressed The Educator's hull with fingers oily from assembling a Christmas order of Schwinn bicycles. Across three reddening knuckles were scrawled the words "ho! ho! ho!", a home-cooked deterrent/physical threat for any member of "stray dog scourge" in search of an unwarranted Christmas discount.

Looking through his shambling window, Simpsey could make out the thin silhouette of a boy, standing with his back to a red Georgia sun, and tossing back and forth what looked to be the other half of the brick that had, moments ago, taken up residency in his storefront window pane.

Laney Mack, swaddled in a weathered leather jacket once owned by his brother, playfully tossed the other half of the brick back and forth, from one hand to the other. His dark brown hair was greased back into a sort-of pompadour. A makeshift necklace of ceramic Christmas lights (courtesy of a strand that had lined the awning over Simpsey's store entrance) kept his neck company.

With deep red bells ringing in his head and his blood pressure barometer beginning to crack like the glass in his storefront window, Simpsey curled his tongue around a swarm of profanities and launched them toward Laney Mack. Though they would burrow into the ears of the occasional passerby and become the spark for the following morning's barber and beauty shop gossip, the words, with all their fangs and fury, would not stir Laney, whose ears had heard much worse in his 16 years, from men with sharper tongues and harder fists.

"Son, you throw that, and the only lights you gonna see this Christmas are the spinning blue kind," Simpsey said, shifting his weight, his thick fingers rhythmically tapping The Educator's hull.

"Seen 'em before, mister," Laney said, scratching his hip. "Seen 'em plenty. I'll be right here, waitin'."

Laney sat down on the curb, he could feel his tailbone ache, still sore from a childhood incident. He rolled his left jean leg up to match his right and looked across the street. A young dog — its coat, a patchwork of frayed fur and bare skin — stared back at him with eyes of two different colors, one a blue tint, the other black as pitch. The dog quivered and paused once aware of Laney's presence, and his starving skin was drawn over ribs that pushed through the sides of his body, bending, bowing out like prison bars made of bone.

Simpsey could feel the anger, scaly and swelling, turning over inside, again and again. He took a firm hold of The Educator and pointed it toward Laney through the hole in his window.

"Do you want me to come out there and show you what I do to dogs like that — dogs like *you* — that come around here and stir up a fuss," he shouted.

Minnie placed her hand on Simpsey's and grazed it with her thumb. She gently removed The Educator from his hand and replaced it with a telephone receiver.

"No need for you two to be sharing the backseat of Hallis' cruiser," she said.

Unblinking and still, Laney scanned the fractured storefront window, the gold "Joy To The World" banner draped beneath the "Bicentennial Christmas Blowout" sign, the fake snowy setting with the rosy-cheeked wax figurine family of carolers on display. He quickly turned his attention to the face of Simpsey Cook, pulpy and enraged, his lips in a snarl, barbed words continuing to fire out of his mouth from behind the cracked glass.

But Laney heard nothing, not a sound. He only saw, in those fractured shards, the reflection of Simpsey Cook, and the faces of other men he had known — men of hard hands and hurtful words.

Tears began to well up in Laney's eyes, and in one swift movement, he scooped up the half brick resting at his feet, and with every ounce of energy in his slight sixteen-year-old frame, hurled it at what was left of Simpsey Cook's storefront window.

SMASH!!

Laney wiped his throwing hand on his jeans and picked a broken flower off the curb. He looked at it for a moment, grazed the delicate, white velvet texture of its remaining petal with his finger and sat down on the curb cross-legged. As a crop of flashing blue lights grew closer on the horizon, Laney closed his eyes and exhaled in a long, deep sigh beneath the sunset's dying glow.

The gold trim on Sergeant Hallis Rivers' nametag flashed like a lightbulb in the late evening sun. He carefully slipped a set of handcuffs around Laney's slim wrists, and noticed the ghosts of bruises and burns decorating his young forearms.

Rivers' sigh went undetected by Laney's ears as the young man slid his spindly frame into the backseat of the cruiser. A police radio crackled and popped. A series of anonymous voices blurting out random numbers and street names.

The cruiser's engine wheezed to life, and the sound of a dying fanbelt introduced itself.

"Buckle up young'n," Rivers asked, doing his best to suppress a chronic cough that had haunted him since late autumn. "S'cuse me, got a midget in my throat."

Laney reached for the belt buckle, its metal casing scalding to the touch. Something was etched on the chrome siding of the buckle, but Laney couldn't make out the words.

Rivers adjusted the rearview mirror, ceremonially tapped twice the Jesus air freshener wrapped around the radio dial and glanced at Laney, whose pale blue eyes dammed up a sadness and suffering shared by a hundred other boys before him who had warmed that seat.

"Not much of a way for a young man to spend Christmas, huh?" Rivers said, adjusting the rearview again. "How old are you?"

"Sixteen," Laney answered in a voice small and quiet, "and spare change."

"Well I take it that spreading holiday cheer wasn't exactly your motivation for throwing a brick through Mr. Cook's window," Rivers said, again trying to keep his nagging cough in check.

"I just wanted a place to stay," Laney said, placing his hand on the belt buckle, which was much cooler now. "Figured jail would be safe, warm. Quiet."

Rivers pulled up to a stoplight and threw the cruiser in park.

"C'mere, you don't need those," he said, motioning for Laney's handcuffs.

Laney rubbed his freed wrists and looked out the window as the light turned green. A little girl wearing a red Rudolph the Red Nosed Reindeer bulb on her nose waved at him from the passenger side window of a pink Mary Kay Cosmetics car, her windy hair all braids and bows. He waved back.

Laney listened to Rivers warble official speak into a walkie talkie, and recognized a few random words: boy, lost, vandalism, grass stains.

Rivers hung up the receiver and looked at the rearview mirror.

"I'm gonna take you into the station for the evening until we get some things squared away, alright?" he directed in a calm tone. "We'll have a cot for you to sleep on, and a couple of roommates for the evening — Henry Bells — don't even get me *started* on that boy; and Reverend Sugars Mandrell, who always volunteers to keep watch over the flock on Christmas Eve. It ain't the Beverly Hills Deluxe, but it'll do. And my wife Evangeline sends in some fine tastin' grub every year, so maybe you'll get a plate full. Sound okay?"

Laney nodded and held his hand up to his nose; he could still smell the flower's fragrant scent.

Rivers looked at the boy briefly once more in the rearview mirror. A part of him wondered how many more like him he'd see in the coming years. Another part wondered how much longer he'd be able to take it.

Inside the Lunsford County Jail, a tabletop Christmas tree, draped in silver tinsel, blinked blue, red, green and purple, and cozied up to a pot of coffee, the steam still rising from its lid like ghosts. A woman's slow molasses croon crackled from a small red radio perched atop the warden's desk and drifted down a warmly lit hallway, its walls decorated with children's Christmas drawings.

Laney's hands were wrapped around two cell bars, and he looked between them to see the drawings — some colored in, others not. One in particular showed a boy with his arms wrapped around members of his family. An orange sun flowered behind them. The image would not shake loose of him.

"I used to draw like that."

Laney turned to track down where the words were coming from.

An old black man, dressed in a black pinstripe suit adorned with a yellow flower pin, smiled at him.

"Except I drew them on automobile hoods, water towers, bathroom stalls," he continued. "I was about your age, too. Just as scrawny."

The holding room's other resident, splayed out on his cot with one boot-covered foot and one bare, remained still, the rising and falling of his chest indicating a state of temporary hibernation.

The old man smiled at Laney, removed his hat and began tapping his red leather shoes on the floor.

"Where you from Little King?" he asked in Laney's direction.

Laney paused and hesitantly shook his head, not knowing to whom the old man was referring.

"You know who Elvis is?"

Laney nodded.

"You kinda look like him," the old man said, picking at the frayed interior of his hat, "so I'ma call you Lil' King."

"I once saw Elvis shoppin' for a Burmese killifish at Jonah Stu's pet store downtown," the other man, now slowly waking, chimed in, stretching his arms toward the ceiling and slipping his Uni-Oil '76 cap snug over his head. "Never liked Elvis, though. More of a Stones man."

The cap's bill was pulled down over the man's brow, so Laney couldn't see his eyes, but he noticed that he had no front teeth.

"So why you in here, King?" the old man continued. "Your momma know where you are?"

Laney glanced between the bars again and looked at the drawings on the wall.

"My momma's gone."

The old man slowly nodded, tapped his foot again to some mystery rhythm playing in his head.

"Your Daddy gone too?"

Laney hesitated a moment before answering.

"Might as well be," he said, running his hand through his makeshift pompadour.

"I see," the old man softly trailed off. "So why you here?"

"I needed a place to stay," Laney answered, slowly slipping off his leather jacket. "To sleep."

The napping man with the Uni-Oil hat flicked up the bill on his cap, revealing a look of disbelief.

Sugars Mandrell leaned out of the dark corner, stretching his long gaunt frame until he was almost face to face with Laney. He tapped his red leather shoes on the floor three times.

"Young man, I'm lookin' at you, and I'm hearin' the words tip-toe out of your mouth, and I'm *knowin'* you're looking for more than just a place to stay and sleep."

Laney could see his own reflection in the old man's eyes. They were fathomless but comforting.

"I see a stray dog in you son," Sugars continued. "It's in every man standing in this room — you, me, even Henry Bells over there. The thing about a stray is this: they always movin' from one doorstep to the next — *always* movin', *always* in search of . . . but always *hungry*."

Sugars moved his face closer to Laney, his eyes growing wider.

"I know you're scared, Little King, and I know you're hungry, but sooner or later you got to be still and *eat*."

Henry Bells sat up from his former reclining position and rested his chin on his knee.

"What'd you do to get yourself in this predicament?" he asked.

"I threw a brick through a store window," Laney answered.

"Which store?"

"Cook's Dimestore Dream."

Sugars shook his head and slipped his hat back on while Henry exploded in laughter.

"They ought to give you the key to the city, son," Henry said through hoarse waves of laughter, wiping his brow with his forearm. "As far as I'm concerned, you've already done your community service."

Laney removed his leather jacket and looked at Henry.

"How'd you get in here?"

Henry slipped off his cap and ran his hands through his thinning, black hair. Two lambchop-sized sideburns crept down the sides of his face and connected to a handlebar mustache prematurely peppered with flecks of gray.

"Well, I realize this ain't exactly the appropriate yuletide tale for this evening," he said, "but I woke up early this morning in the middle of that unpaved access road that intersects Cynthiana. I was messed up, to be honest. Just tore up. The headache, the bruises from a couple of unfriendly dalliances from the evening prior — the whole bit. I was on my back and opened my right hand; there was a note all scrunched up; it read "look in your back left jeans pocket for a Christmas surprise." The knuckles on my left hand were still busted, but I shoved it into my back left pocket and pulled out a little ziplock bag — with two of my front teeth inside.

Henry flashed a huge gap-toothed grin. Sugars and Laney both laughed.

"That's my story young man. Public intoxication was my ticket to these deluxe accommodations I share with you tonight."

Sugars shook his head.

"What did you do with your teeth," Laney asked, his smile unable to come undone.

"I sent 'em to my stepfather, wrapped up in a bow all nice and pretty. Slipped a note inside that read"*Somebody else got to me before you did — Merry Christmas.*"

The sound of Hallis Rivers' 1964 Udelia High class ring repeatedly tick-tacking against one of the cell bars interrupted another round of laughter.

"Alright gentlemen," he said, slipping three paper boxes through a slot in the cell door, "Evangeline wanted to make sure all 'overnight residents' went to bed this Christmas Eve on a full stomach, so here are the goods: ham sandwiches, homemade biscuits, chocolate chip & pecan cookies. Got a quart of sweet tea to wash it down, too."

A chorus of thank you's chimed out to meet the Warden's generosity.

"What's this, the third Christmas Eve in a row Henry?" Hallis asked, cocking an eyebrow. "We gonna have to officially christen this the Henry Bells Holding Tank #3?"

"It's Evangeline's fault, son," he answered, smiling. "Her cooking's too damn good — drive a man to a life of crime."

After Rivers wished all a Merry Christmas, and continued his mission toward a half-empty coffee pot, Sugars poured three even cups of sweet tea and asked if Henry and Laney would stand with him to say a prayer before dinner.

As the three men stood together, arms interlocked and heads bowed, Laney opened one eye and looked again, through the cell bars, to the drawing of the family on the wall, their faces smiling, their arms wrapped around each other.

He felt a squeeze from Sugar's hand.

"Lord, may these stray sons finally find their way, be at peace — and eat," he said, finishing up his prayer.

"Though I am here tonight as a shepherd, I am also one of the flock. Amen."

Sugars kneeled down, removed the yellow flower from his coat and pinned it on Laney's leather jacket.

"Every stray dog needs a place to be still and belong," the old man said. "Tonight, Little King, you among family."

A smile slid across Laney's face, and his eyes shifted focus from the welcoming embrace of the old man's eyes to the Christmas drawing, posted on the wall outside the jail cell — the same one that had caught his attention upon his arrival.

Looking at the drawing — a crude, crayon image of what looked like a boy wrapping his arms around his family — gave Laney a strange feeling, like when a thunderstorm sometimes cracks the sky open on a sunny summer day.

Biting into one of Evangeline's biscuits, Laney squinted his eyes in an effort to read the words inscribed on the bottom of the drawing. He squinted harder, his eyes reaching out like hands from between the bars. He squinted until his head hurt, but the words were just out of reach.

15

THE MERCY SEAT

"That's right Jethro. Day after tomorrow, you'll be ridin' that roller-coaster straight to hell!" Elroy Perkins shouted, raising his voice like an old-time evangelist preaching his last night at a dirt-road revival. "And it'll be one hot ride." Of course, Elroy was no evangelist. He was the kind of man who made sport of disabled children and prison rape victims, and had no idea what joy or happiness felt like. The closest Elroy could come was to experience a kind of perverted pleasure in response to the pain and suffering of others, and the most genuine smile he could muster always ended up looking like a sneer.

The object of Elroy's tirade responded with a series of low moans and muffled sobs. Jethro curled up on his prison cot and tried to block out the taunts, but like all the other times, the ridicule seeped through the fingers that covered his ears and touched the fear deep within him. Elroy had his number.

"Jethro's" real name was Gerald. He was from the red clay hill country of North Georgia. Twenty-six years old and a petty criminal since he was fourteen, Gerald had been housed in Section D of the Row for a little over seven years. His most recent incarceration was the result of an incident involving him and his two older cousins, Alvin and Earl. During a night of drinking and big talk, they had come upon a high school couple having a romantic interlude in the back seat of a Ford Taurus on Hollow Leg Ridge. With the boldness that only alcohol can provide, Gerald and his cousins robbed the couple. When the boy, Lester Johnson, an All-State tight end for the local high school had resisted, they killed him and raped his girlfriend, Wanda Jean, leaving her naked and delirious on a frigid October night. Gerald was the only one who received the death sentence, compliments of his cousins turning state's evidence and the inadequacy of his court appointed attorney.

If the truth were known, Gerald was a follower, not a leader. He never initiated anything, but was always ready to go along for the ride, and more often than not, as evidenced by his numerous juvenile court appearances, he rarely knew where the ride was going. In fact, on the night in question, Gerald wet his pants at the sight of Wanda Jean being sexually assaulted by his cousins. He remained a virgin, although no one, especially the jury, believed him. Someone had to pay for the death of Lester and the rape of Wanda Jean and Alvin and Earl decided to elect Gerald. Barely able to read and burdened with an unmistakable hillbilly accent, Gerald had been renamed Jethro by his twelve fellow boarders on Section D of death row at the State Prison. Day after tomorrow, he was going to take a final ride, as Elroy had so cruelly put it. And for once, he knew where the ride was going.

Elroy was Jethro's chief tormenter on death row. Although Elroy was his birth name, he hated it. He wished his name was Elvis, like the King of Rock and Roll. Elroy saw himself as a ladies' man and a general all-around bad boy. He often addressed other men not by their given name but by the term "Honcho," or "Cacaos," or "Chief." And Elroy was more than a little proud of the crude tattoo scrawled the length of his left forearm. It read "Bad to the Bone," and few who knew him would disagree.

He had previously served twelve years in prison for beating to death the man who had taken up with his former girlfriend. Three days after he was released from prison, he killed his ex-girlfriend and was sentenced to death. He had bragged before and after he killed her that "No woman leaves Elroy T. Perkins and lives to tell about it." Of course, many had throughout Elroy's life, starting with his Mother, Eunice, when he was six years old.

There had been other assaults, physical and sexual, in Elroy's past that he had not been charged with—usually due to intimidation and on occasion, dumb luck. Elroy's Grandmother had raised him and had been heard to say on more than one occasion that Elroy himself was, more or less, an assault on the human race. Her words turned out to be prophetic. Elroy rarely passed on an opportunity to insult or harass anyone he came in contact with. When he wasn't targeting other inmates or the occasional correctional officer for abuse, he lay on his cot and sulked. While the other inmates had backed off hassling Jethro, who on a good day was an easy target for ridicule and laughter, Elroy, instead, turned up the heat.

When a death row inmate was nearing his execution date, a strange kind of solidarity encompassed his death row compatriots. Even occasional words of encouragement could be heard coming from one cell or another in the long, hot nights leading up the designated man's final walk. It was a reverent, unspoken tradition on death row—a kind of "don't speak ill of the one who is about to be dead." Of course, Elroy didn't observe traditions—especially ones that deprived him of the simple pleasures found in tormenting the doomed and the damned.

Lost in his own thoughts, a middle-aged man with a slight paunch and graying temples turned from the small window he was looking through, and faced his night shift partner, Officer Ed Jenkins, who was clearly agitated.

"The boy's carrying-on is unsettling the other men. Things are getting a little dicey. You think we ought to try to put a lid on that asshole Elroy and maybe calm the kid down? The Doc's done given him all the "meds" he's gonna get until tomorrow."

Popping a fresh stick of chewing gum in his mouth, he looked at Ed Jenkins and replied, "I'll see what I can do."

That's really how it all started. Up until that moment, Cleve Jefferson, known by many as Bishop, was just another inmate waiting on death in Section D.

Although most men on any death row are usually low-keyed to the point of being docile, there are always one or two Elroys to contend with. Sometimes the trouble-makers are mentally ill, but there are others like Elroy who are just plain mean. Of course, the former doesn't necessarily exclude the latter. One could be both mean and crazy.

The only way to deal with a primitive like Elroy was to make clear to him that the pain you were going to cause him was substantially greater than the pleasure he was experiencing. For Elroy, it was the threat of having his one hour a day on the small, interior exercise yard taken from him. To make sure he got the point, Sergeant J.T. Jones added the possibility that his canteen privileges would be suspended for a month. The threat of no Cokes, candy, or Little Debby snack cakes drove Elroy pouting to his cot in the corner of his cell.

Elroy's bullshit was contained in short order. Jethro's fragile grasp on reality proved to be another matter. What Elroy had put in motion seemed to have taken on a life of its own as Jethro's moans turned to wailing and left him curled up in a fetal position on the floor of his cell. Ed Jenkins was getting more than a little concerned.

"What are we gonna do, Sarge?"

"I'm not sure, Ed," J.T. Jones answered. "One thing I do know is that if we wake Major Dawson from his evening nap at Central Control, there will be hell to pay. I think I'll take one more shot at trying to calm him down."

J.T. Jones tried to talk to Jethro in his most soothing voice, but his crying intensified and brought curses and shouts for quiet from the other inmates who were trying to sleep.

"All right son," J.T. said to himself as much as anyone else. "I guess I'll go wake up the Major."

As he walked down the corridor to his office, a voice called out to him from cell 11. "Sergeant Jones."

J.T. stopped and walked back to Bishop's cell.

A small, bald black man with long, gray sideburns looked at him intently. "I believe I could help the young man."

"And how would you do that?" J.T. asked, picking something out of his ear.

"Me and him have been talking a lot during the last few days. I've been praying for him and I believe he might listen to me."

"Thanks for your offer, Bishop, but I doubt Jethro would listen to anybody in his present state. And with what's facing him day after tomorrow, I can't say as I blame him. Anyway, you're three cells down from him—not close enough to carry on much of a conversation."

Bishop sat down on his cot and smiled.

"Sergeant, I can't help you with the cell arrangements, but I can help you with Gerald."

J.T. looked at Bishop for a moment, then shook his head and walked back to his office.

"Good God! You can't be serious," Ed exclaimed. "We could be fired!"

"Not if you keep your mouth shut," J.T. replied, popping a fresh stick of gum in his mouth.

"If anything goes wrong, I'll take the blame."

"Damn straight you will!" Ed responded. "If the shit hits the fan, I'm deaf, dumb and blind."

As J.T. unlocked Bishop's cell door, he was amused that Bishop didn't seem to be surprised by his actions. With his tattered Bible in hand, Bishop proceeded to the chair J.T. had placed next to the condemned man's cell.

J.T. positioned himself where he could maintain a clear vision, while allowing Bishop and Jethro some measure of privacy. As Bishop pressed his face against the bars of Jethro's cell door, J.T. clearly heard only one word during his thirty-minute vigil.

"Gerald."

Even after all these years, J.T. was still amazed at the effect that one word had on the delirious young man. At the single utterance of his name, Jethro's body relaxed and he grew silent. Bishop said nothing, but sat and waited. From his vantage point J.T. could see Jethro sit up within a few minutes of Bishop's greeting and crawl on his hands and knees toward the small, black man with the long gray sideburns. What followed were whispers that sounded like praying. First Bishop, then Jethro. Then Bishop passed his Bible through the bars to the young prisoner and they clasped hands in silence, simply looking at each other for a time. Finally, Bishop smiled at Jethro, rose to his feet and walked back to the front of his cell. Once J.T. had locked the door behind him, Bishop turned and looked at him with quiet approval.

"Thank you, Sergeant Jones."

Nodding his head, J.T. went to check on Jethro and found him curled up on his cot, his face pressed against Bishop's Bible. Jethro looked up at the Sergeant for a brief moment, but said nothing and then closed his eyes.

Walking back to the office, Sergeant J.T. Jones experienced a strange sensation. He felt light-headed. Jethro's look had unsettled him and he had the strange feeling that on that particular night it was Bishop, and not him, who was in control of his domain. J.T. was grateful for the steaming cup of coffee Ed offered him.

Two days later, Jethro was executed.

Cleve Jefferson, who came to be known on death row as "Bishop," never denied his guilt. He had been a small-time drug dealer who killed two rivals in a shoot-out. That act alone would not have put him on death row—even with the list of other crimes and drug-related assaults on his rap sheet. Cleve's ticket to death row came as a result of his accidentally shooting Maria Lopez, a single mother with two young children during the same shoot-out.

During his first two years on the row, he had been an angry young man, ranting against a racist justice system and filing endless appeals. Then one day, without explanation, Cleve Jefferson gradually became less belligerent and less talkative. As he began to withdraw, Doc Hansen assumed he was experiencing the kind of depression typical for death row inmates and offered him anti-depressants, which he politely refused. Soon after, he quit talking altogether.

For six months Cleve Jefferson said nothing. He slept, ate and sat on the edge of his cot, staring at the picture of Maria Lopez he had torn out of a newspaper. From time to time deep in the night, sobbing could be heard coming from his cell. Correctional officers on all three shifts pooled their money to see who would correctly guess the night Cleve Jefferson would take his life.

On New Year's Day of his third year on death row, Cleve Jefferson began to talk again. Over the next two years, he collected and read a variety of religious and holy books, including the Bible, the Koran, the Ramayana, the Tao Te Ching, the Tibetan Book of the Dead and Black Elk Speaks. Although Cleve seemed to prefer the Bible or his "Grandmama's Book" as he referred to it, he read and studied a wide variety of religious and wisdom traditions. He also began to share his readings and thoughts with anyone on the row who would listen. Most didn't, but a few did. Those few seemed intrigued with what he had to say and began to refer to Cleve as "Bishop." Over the years, everyone—officer and inmate alike—came to refer to him as Bishop as much out of habit as anything else. Most of the officers figured Cleve had gone a little crazy, but accepted that the men on death row coped with their predicament in different ways as best they could.

The only non-inmate who would talk with Cleve about spiritual matters was a good-natured, young Chaplain who seemed to genuinely enjoy their conversations. His two favorite expressions to Bishop were "I go to three years of Seminary to become a Reverend and you go to death row and end up a Bishop" and "I'll convert you to a Baptist yet." Each time Chaplain Smith would utter either of those phrases, Bishop's response was always the same—a smile and a chuckle. Bishop had been on death row for ten years when he thanked Sergeant J.T. Jones for letting him talk to Jethro. After that night, everything changed.

At first, their chats would only last ten or fifteen minutes, usually in the wee hours of the morning while the other inmates were asleep and Ed Jenkins was doing paperwork. Gradually, fifteen-minute chats evolved into one to two hour conversations between two men, separated by prison bars, race and a lifetime of different experiences. Their conversations ranged from prison life to sports to religion or whatever else caught their fancy. J.T. would sit in a folding chair with his coffee cup and thermos and Bishop on the edge of his cot, finishing the last of the sweet potato pie J.T. had slipped him, compliments of Margie, J.T.'s wife of twenty years.

J.T. Jones was not a particularly sentimental man. He honored the obligatory birthdays and other holidays with friendly resolve. He wasn't against such occasions any more than he was against going to the Methodist church with his wife on most Sunday mornings. Such traditions just didn't hold much appeal for him. J.T. seemed to find more solace walking in the woods on the farm that had been his Daddy's before it was his and his Granddaddy's before that. Only the occasional bird in flight could hear him singing the hymns of his youth while he pole fished from the banks of the old mill pond on the back side of his farm.

It wasn't so much that J.T. Jones was a simple man, but more that his needs and wants were simple. He had driven the same pick-up truck for the last twelve years and for the most part, lived his life from the inside out. He was a careful and practical man who was at the same time, curious in a quiet sort of a way. And when a situation called for it he was willing to go against convention and take a chance. It was a mix of the three—curiosity, inwardness and nonconformity that drew J.T. to Bishop.

J.T.'s practical and careful nature required that he first review the file and background of the man who had come to be known as Bishop. The conclusion had been clear. Cleve Jefferson had become Bishop through some sort of gradual transformation, which in itself was not that uncommon on death row. J.T. had witnessed a number of men experience genuine religious conversions when facing death. Getting one's house in order, seeking some sense of forgiveness for the harm that one has done, and looking for hope in a better life beyond the grave—a fresh start so to speak—was understandable to J.T. What was different about Bishop in comparison to the others was that he didn't seem to follow any particular tradition. He didn't claim to be a Baptist, Methodist, Catholic, or Muslim. All

J.T. ever heard him refer to himself as when he conversed with other inmates, was that he was one of "God's boys." In fact, every morning, seven days a week, when breakfast was served, Bishop always issued forth the same greeting to the residents of death row, Section D: "How are God's boys this morning?"

The responses to his daily query were varied and ranged from silence to complimentary replies, and on occasion, expletive-laced retorts from inmates like Elroy. J.T. smiled as he recalled a particular breakfast exchange between Bishop and Elroy, who had awaken in a particularly foul mood.

"Damn God's boys and damn you, you no-account Nigger!" snarled Elroy. "You were born a Nigger and you'll die a Nigger. A Nigger is all you'll ever be."

After the course of profanities, which echoed from other inmates toward Elroy subsided, Bishop simply chuckled and responded in a clear, calm voice.

"You're more right than you know, Elroy. I was a Nigger just as you are. We're all Niggers until we sit in the mercy seat. It's only through the mercy seat that Niggers like you and me can become men in this world and children of God."

Of course, Elroy didn't agree with Bishop's assessment and let him know in no uncertain terms before returning to his cot.

Eventually, the residents of Section D seemed to look forward to rather than tolerate Bishop's early morning greeting. J.T. and the other officers began to sense a kind of respect and even affection on the part of the other inmates toward the old man.

Numerous helpings of sweet potato pie, cooked greens and homemade cornbread later, J.T. Jones finally got around to asking Bishop the questions he had been curious about for a long time.

Handing Bishop a fresh cup of coffee through the bars, J.T. paused before he spoke.

"Bishop, exactly what kind of religious man are you? You say you are one of God's boys, but what does that mean? You got all these books about different religions and such, but you've never said what your religion is—only that you are one of God's boys."

J.T. stopped talking and took a long sip of his coffee.

"That's a pretty long question, Sergeant. Anything else?"

"Yeah, what's the 'mercy seat'?" J.T. asked, warming his hands on his coffee cup.

Bishop closed his eyes and sat quietly before answering. Finally, he spoke.

"I've read, prayed and meditated on the holy books of many faiths. The reason I keep coming back to the Bible is because it's my Grandmama's book. She called it the 'Good Book.' To me, it's 'Grandmama's Book.' You know, she raised me for the first eight years of my life, before she died of the consumption. Sitting on her front porch in the late afternoon after she had returned from working in the fields, we would drink mason jars filled with strong, sweet tea. Every afternoon, my Grandmama would read to me from the 'Good Book' and tell me stories about Jesus and the Holy Ghost. Sometimes her stories would lift me up beyond the clouds and other times they'd scare the pure hell out of me. She was a small woman with a big faith I didn't understand at the time."

Bishop paused to take a sip of coffee.

"After all my praying, reading and studying, I can't really say I know all that much 'bout anything. What I can say is that I love the Jesus my Grandmama taught me about. I guess you could say that I think of myself as a 'Jesus Man' who has a lot of friends and relatives from other faiths."

"Chaplain Smith, of course, doesn't agree," Bishop said, chuckling. "He says all my friends and relatives are going straight to hell."

Bishop drank the last of his coffee and smiled. "I like him. He's a young man with good intentions and a lot of back roads left to travel."

J.T. refilled Bishop's extend cup with coffee from his thermos. "Tell me about the 'mercy seat.'"

Bishop closed his eyes once again and grew quiet. J.T. sipped his coffee in silence and waited.

"When I was dealing drugs, violence was a way of life—nothing special. Intimidation, beatings and sexual assaults, even murder—nothing special. And then the shooting—nothing new, except this time, I killed a single mother in the crossfire. Left two small children behind. I'd seen innocent people hurt—even killed, but never by my hand."

"From the time I saw her picture at the trial, I became affected in a way that's hard to explain. It's like I was haunted. I cut that dead woman's picture out of the newspaper and carried it with me. At night, I'd dream that my Grandmama was looking at me, tears streaming from her eyes. During the day, I found myself either looking at the picture of the woman that I killed or thinking about her two children."

"When I arrived here on death row, I taped Maria Lopez's picture on the wall at the end of my cot. Then I wrote my cousin, Angela, and asked her to send me my Grandmama's Bible. Felt like I was going crazy, staring at that picture of Maria Lopez all day and dreaming about my Grandmama all night."

"When my Grandmama's 'Good Book' came in the mail, things began to change. As I began to read and to pray, I stopped dreaming about her. Then I quit talking and ate very little."

J.T. interjected, "We thought you were losing it—had you on 24 hour suicide watch."

"All I was concerned about was the picture on my wall and the hot ball of pain that was filling up my insides. I felt like I couldn't breathe . . . felt like I was on fire. And then one night while I was looking at that photograph, that ball of fire exploded and buried me alive in its ashes."

A thin bead of sweat broke out on Bishop's forehead.

"I felt her suffering as she drew her last breath. I felt the sorrow of her children losing their mother. I felt the loss of her parents and friends. I even felt the pain of my own

Mama abandoning me when I was a little boy. It was like I was responsible for everything bad that had happened to anybody and everybody. I couldn't bear it. I was drowning in a sea of sorrow. After there were no tears left for me to cry, I began to pray to the Lord Almighty for forgiveness—for deliverance from who I was and what I had become."

"Then the big change happened."

Bishop grew quiet once more as his eyes filled with tears.

J.T. inquired softly, "What was the big change?"

In a choked voice, Bishop replied, "I finally got to sit in the 'mercy seat.' I was crying, praying, meditating and looking at that picture. I don't know how long I had been at it. I had no sense of time—it was like I was outside of time. All I know is what happened next.

"As I looked at that picture, the face of Maria Lopez began to change. Her face began to change into the face of a person I had never seen before. But I knew who it was. It was in the eyes. Not like the pictures on those funeral parlor fans. Different, like peeling off the skin to see what it hid. I been mistaking the peeling for the fruit. Those eyes were the fruit—what's behind the behind. It was Him.

"I wanted to look away, but I couldn't. Kept looking at that picture for I don't know how long. Then it changed back . . . changed back to the face of the woman I killed. That picture was like a magnet. Couldn't take my eyes off it. And then . . . Oh Lord . . . and then . . .

"The picture spoke to me. Maria Lopez's picture spoke to me."

Once again, Bishop fell silent, his head bowed.

"What did it say?" J.T. asked in a hushed tone.

Bishop looked at J.T. a long time before speaking. "She said, 'I died so that you might live.'"

Neither man spoke for a long time, each lost in his own thoughts.

Finally, Bishop took a deep breath and dried his eyes with the back of his hand. "The mercy seat's about second chances—about being forgiven when forgiveness isn't possible. Having your heart broken into a thousand pieces—then opened up and made new again."

"You got any of that coffee left?" Bishop queried with a weary smile.

Taking a swallow of the hot coffee, he continued, "If I've learned one thing from what I experienced, it's that I don't know much of anything. But—thank the Lord—I do know about the mercy seat."

Bishop's appeals finally ran out. He had plenty of letters of support, including one from J.T. and Chaplain Smith. They weren't asking for the moon, just that his sentence be commuted to life without parole, but it was an election year and everyone knows that mercy takes a back seat on election years.

The morning Bishop was transferred to the death-watch cell, J.T. came in even though it was his day off. He came in to say goodbye. It was the last time they sat together, he in his folding chair and Bishop on the edge of his cot.

Bishop looked at him and smiled. "J.T., I guess this is it. It's all she wrote for this ol' world."

No inmate before or since ever called J.T. by his first name, but on that morning Bishop did and to J.T., it seemed only natural.

All he could say in response was, "I guess so."

He often wished his response had been more helpful, more encouraging, but that's all J.T. said—"I guess so."

Then Bishop had a final request for him, a special favor to ask. He wanted J.T. to make a promise to him.

"Promise me something."

"Promise you what?"

Reaching through the bars, Bishop gently placed his right hand on J.T.'s heart. "Promise me you'll remember that you're also one of God's boys."

J.T. couldn't speak. All he could do was nod his head.

After Bishop's death, J.T. received a package from Angela, Bishop's cousin. She wrote in a short note that Bishop had wanted him to have his Grandmama's 'Good Book.'

Sitting on his front porch, he looked at the book in his lap and smelled the supper Margie was cooking.

Opening the front screen door, Margie peered out at her husband.

"Honey, what you thinking about?"

"I'm thinking about this book—and that I'm grateful for you and the life I've had. But as grateful as I am, one thing is as certain as the sun setting over that grove of poplar trees—I miss my friend."

16

VIRGIL'S SOLACE

T he eighteen-wheeler bellowed and belched its way down Highway 33 through the cracked, black two-lane yellow pine forests. Six miles this side of "Joe Wheeler's Barbecue Palace", Eugene McReady did what he had done three times a week for the last seven years. He looked to his left at the small unpainted clapboard farmhouse perched on what passed for a hill in southwest Tennessee and pulled his horn for three short bursts.

Virgil Murdock sat where he always did--third step from the bottom that led to the covered porch of the house he shared with Amos and Margie-Lee Murdock, his father and mother. To the occasional visitor, Virgil seemed to sit "at attention," as though he were waiting for some hidden command, or marching orders. His posture wasn't one of relaxed repose or whimsical self-reflection. Rigid and stoic, Virgil looked as though he were leaning into his silence in anticipation of something unseen but still felt–some faint dread or unwelcome visitation. His gaze remained steady throughout the day, placed just above the treeline's horizon on the other side of highway 33, the only exception was occasional furtive glances toward the creek and woods down the hill to his right. Those brief interruptions looked to his parents like momentary distractions from his primary meditation—sometimes accompanied by the slightest hint of pleasantness; other times followed by a fearful stare.

Sitting at attention on his step of preference, Virgil waited patiently for three events around which his solitary existence revolved—his father's return from work at the sawmill, his mother calling him for lunch or supper, and Eugene McReady's greeting and acknowledgment which arrived three times a week.

The horn's three short blasts turned Virgil's head. His eyes and the corners of his mouth crinkled into the closest thing to a smile anyone in Elbert County would see from Virgil except for when his father rubbed his back each evening after supper.

There had been a brief period of time three years ago when Amos and Margie-Lee's spirits had soared at the possibility of a miracle.

Their hope began when Eugene McReady parked his eighteen wheeler on the shoulder of the road just past Murphy's General Store in order to purchase a Coca Cola and a bologna and cheese sandwich for his lunch. While waiting to order, he overheard the store's owner, Red Murphy, and two elderly patrons talking about Virgil's state of mind.

"I tell you, the boy ain't been right since the war," Red exclaimed as he poked a fresh-cut wedge of Red Man chewing tobacco into his mouth.

"I ain't so sure 'bout that, Red. As I think back, Virgil was always a little strange. Even when he was a boy--- I can remember some peculiarities like the time..."

" Shut your mouth, Peety Matthews," shouted a large bald-headed man in worn denim overalls, pointing his finger at the smaller man. "You callin' anybody peculiar's like the pot calling the kettle black. Besides, Virgil's a veteran. He served his country for the likes of you and me and paid one hell of a price! He's up there sitting on those steps reliving all that terror while me and you are down here with Red, sipping colas and eatin' candy bars. You ought to be ashamed of yourself."

Peety's face turned crimson. "I didn't mean no disrespect, I was just speaking my mind."

J.D. ground out the butt of his hand-rolled cigarette in the ashtray on the counter.

"No disrespect, my ass," he scoffed. If you spoke your mind like that on Wednesday evenings when Amos comes by for his weekly game of checkers with Red, he'd throw your scrawny behind out in the street."

"Now boys, settle down," Red chimed in, spitting a stream of tobacco juice into an empty Maxwell House coffee can on the floor. "We've got a customer here who needs waitin' on."

The two old-timers looked at the newcomer and returned to their seats around the warmth of the potbellied stove. For a time, the only sounds were the popping of the stove's hot sheet metal as Eugene ate his lunch.

Finally, Red broke the silence.

"I noticed you been stoppin' from time to time. Where you haulin' all that produce?"

Pausing between mouthfuls of bologna and cheese, Eugene took a long drink of Coca Cola before responding.

"Got me a new route. Three times a week to the train depot at Higgsville. From there I reckon they ship the produce to Memphis and beyond."

Eugene finished the last of his cold drink and placed the empty bottle on the counter.

"Sorry to hear about the fellow who's having trouble."

Red's eyes narrowed slightly. "Yeah, it's a shame."

"Yeah, it is. There's a lot of folks who came back like..."

"His name's Virgil," Red interjected.

"Truth is, I was a lot like Virgil the first year I got back. Couldn't sleep. Drank too much. Nightmares. Stuff like that."

J.D and Peety roused out of their collective sulking and perked up. Clearing his throat, Red relaxed a bit and looked squarely at Eugene.

"Where did you serve?"

Lost in a moment's reflection, Eugene replied softly, "Infantry...two years in Europe. Where did Virgil serve?"

J.D rose to his feet and approached Eugene, followed by a subdued Peety.

"Virgil served in Europe too. Fought in the Battle of the Bulge. Krauts overran his unit. Him and one other fella were the only ones who survived."

" That was one hell of a fight. Lot of good men died. But then, a lot of good men always die in war."

J.D. extended his hand to Eugene.

"Were you at the Bulge?"

Eugene took J.D.'s hand.

"Yeah, I was at Bastogne."

J.D. became more animated. "Did you know Virgil? Matter o' fact, I lost a cousin in that battle. Name of Eli Givins. You ever hear of him?

"Don't believe I knew Virgil or Eli. Things were crazy. The whole time was kind of a blur. Don't remember a lot of details. Some that I do remember, I wish I didn't."

Red sighed. "After Virgil recovered from his wounds, they assigned him to the burial detail. All them poor boys—their bodies stacked like cordwood—it was too much for Virgil. He went downhill from there. They ended shipping him to a Veteran's hospital down in Louisiana. He wasn't right in his mind. Amos couldn't get off work at the sawmill so his poor Mama had to go all the way to Louisiana and fetch him herself."

A thin bead of sweat broke out on Eugene's forehead.

Bodies....stacked....cordwood. Eugene felt a rush of the past blow by him. The room seemed uncomfortably warm. He looked at his watch, then at the three older men.

"Fellas, it's been nice meeting you. I got to get on down to Higgsville with my load. Be sure to give Virgil and his family my best."

Red and Peety spoke in unison, "Same to you...."

"Name's Eugene."

As he turned to leave, Red tossed a Hershey bar to him. "It's on the house."

That's how it started—how Amos and Margie-Lee began to hope in the possibility that their son might one day return from no-man's-land. And for the first month or two, their dreams of rescue like the promise of the coming spring, held them breathless.

From their first meeting, the two men hit it off. Perhaps, it was a tilt of the head or a hint of the haunted memories that combat veterans share. Whatever it was, Eugene and Virgil quickly progressed from "how do you do's" to more private conversations sitting on the front steps of Murphy's store while Red and Virgil's father played checkers inside under the watchful eyes of Peety and J.D. The four men marveled at how Eugene McReady drew Virgil out. Checkers became an excuse for them to gather and listen in reverence for the rustle of salvation in the evening breeze. Eugene, the shepherd, guiding Virgil, the wounded, lost sheep back to the fold. They strained to listen for the sounds of Virgil's return from the land of the lost and the dead. The four men's whispers were like children's prayers, claiming the magical return of their beloved. The high point of their Wednesday evening vigil was the night they heard Virgil laugh for the first time since he returned from the war. He was like the Virgil of old, laughing spontaneously from deep within his belly. The four men held their breathe, rapt in wonder and awe at the sound of such a thing.

And then, as quickly as Virgil had stepped forward into the light, he retreated back into the shadows of his past.

Red poured a cup of coffee and handed it to Eugene.

"I still can't believe Virgil quit showing up on Wednesdays. Seemed like he was coming out of his slump. 'Specially after we heard him laugh that one night. That was sure enough a sound for sore ears."

Eugene sipped the hot coffee.

"Yeah, I know what you mean. Coming back from the likes of what Virgil saw can be a tricky business. Had a fella in my platoon from Texas by the name of Roman Gidensky. We all called him Romeo. He got hit by a piece of shrapnel from a German 88 and was carted off to the field hospital. He seemed fine when he returned, joking with everybody and showing off his Purple Heart. One morning out of the blue, Romeo just shut down. Nobody knew why. He wouldn't talk to anybody, even the company commander. He just sat looking at his purple heart, smoking one cigarette after another."

Red reached for the coffee pot.

"What happened to your friend?"

Eugene stuck his cup out for a refill.

"Don't know. Never heard from him again."

The two men drank their coffee in silence and listened to the sound of a tractor turning the soil for spring planting in a nearby field.

Virgil's retreat found Amos and Margie-Lee slipping back into their routine as before only sadder. Virgil spent most of his day sitting at attention, third step from the bottom, watching for the ghosts in the woods. He listened patiently for Margie-Lee's mealtime commands and Eugene's thrice weekly horn-blowing salutes. More than anything else though, Virgil listened for the sound of his Daddy's footsteps creaking their way across the weathered front porch after supper and his tender touch that followed.

Amos rubbed his son's back and shoulders with strong hands, carefully kneading and loosening the knots of tension and fear. Virgil would occasionally exhale a low moan as his body relaxed from the pressure of his father's practiced fingers. During the countless hours Amos massaged the tightness out of his son's back and shoulders, he found himself imagining that his hands held magical powers—that he could apply that same, strong delicate touch to Virgil's broken mind and spirit.

"Did you hear from Eugene today? Red said he's letting his boy, Eddie, ride with him when he makes his run to Higgsville."

"Yessir. Three blows of the horn, same as usual."

Amos stopped momentarily to fish the Prince Albert can out of his sweat-stained khakis and rolled himself a cigarette.

"That Eugene's a fine fellow."

Amos lit his cigarette and resumed rubbing Virgil's back. Virgil looked toward the highway and down at the woods.

"You know, Daddy, Eugene's the only person who knows what I went through–what went through me."

Amos flicked the ash from the end of his cigarette and coughed.

Virgil continued when he felt his father's hands return.

"I knew Eugene understood the first night you introduced me to him at Murphy's store. It was in his eyes. A man can't hide that look. He'd like to, but he can't." Virgil's voice trailed off.

Amos patted his son's head, signaling the end of the evening's back-rub.

"Honeysuckle smells good."

It had been a good evening. Father and son together, enjoying a warm summer night, listening to the serenade of the crickets and Margie-Lee, wife of one and Mother to the other, hum "Amazing Grace" while she cleaned up the kitchen.

The following week, Amos was diagnosed with lung cancer.

Six months to the day after Doc Brown's diagnosis, Amos died.

The day before Amos's funeral, Virgil killed himself.

"I shorely do miss Amos," J.D. lamented as he sat on a coca cola crate, leaning against the wall of Murphy's storefront.

"That was one sad sight," Peety groaned in agreement. "Father and son, buried at the same time, side by side. Why in the world would Virgil put the barrel of his Daddy's shotgun in his mouth and pull the trigger in the middle of highway 33?"

Red wiped the summer heat dripping from his brow with the back of his hand.

"Don't have no idea. Poor Margie-Lee. 'Course, she couldn't have managed Virgil by herself. Maybe it was a blessing of sorts."

J.D. stretched his legs out in front of him.

"Maybe so. Or maybe he thought that was the only way he could go a lookin' for his Daddy. Reverend Hamm says Margie-Lee plans to sell the home place and move in with her widowed sister in Tuscaloosa."

Red popped a piece of Juicy Fruit gum in his mouth.

"It's probably for the best."

The eighteen-wheeler leaned into a familiar curve on highway 33 with a roar. Loaded with corn bound for the depot at Higgsville, Eugene watched his son fiddle with the radio.

Eddie looked up at his father and smiled.

"Daddy, can I blow the horn for Virgil?"

Turning to his son, he gently squeezed his shoulder.

"Yes, Eddie. Blow the horn for Virgil."

17

THE END IS NEAR

From a pigeon's vantage point high atop the Mercantile Bank, the mass of people scurrying along the avenue below looked like the tide of some great ocean. There is a certain rhythm and symmetry to the movement of people going to work.

The early morning cadence was quicker and more stiff-legged than the evening quitting time promenade.

Why did they walk that way?

Perhaps their slightly desperate gait was motivated by a fear of being late and the heavy-lidded glances of disapproval that would be sure to follow. Other travelers in the urgent parade may have had a driving desire to be the early bird that gets the worm or at least hold onto the part of the worm they had. The edge they pursued was driven by a caffeine fortified staccato march toward the challenges that lay before them.

In the midst of this swirl of humanity stood an old man with a sign. The cardboard attached to a broom handle stated the message in large red letters: *Repent! The End is Near!*

The sign bearer was tall and gaunt with a long, meticulously groomed white beard. He wore a faded red plaid flannel shirt, blue jeans that had seen better days and white patent leather loafers. Perched on his head was a greasy baseball cap with an American flag pinned one side and a silver cross pinned on the other. His angular face framed deep-set clear blue eyes and wore a somber expression.

The current of men and women swept past him without so much as a glance.

Across the street, three well dressed men in their thirties sat in a café and sipped the remnants of their Starbucks and observed the old man.

The first man said, "He's got to be crazy–standing in the middle of the business district with that goofy sign. Somebody ought to call the police."

The second man replied, "He may be a little off, but I doubt he's dangerous. He probably just wants some attention."

The third man said nothing and continued to sip his coffee.

The first man turned to him.

"Bill, what do think? Is the old man crazy-dangerous or crazy-harmless?"

"Maybe neither."

"Neither," the second man queried. "What kind of answer is that?"

Bill drained the last of his coffee and tossed his cup in the trash can.

"Maybe he knows something we don't."

All three men chuckled at the thought of it.

"Maybe, I'll go ask him."

"You've got to be kidding. That old man may pull a knife on you. You know how unpredictable those kind of people are."

The second man chimed in, "He may even hit you with his sign."

The first and second man laughed, but stopped when they realized Bill was serious.

Bill turned to his two companions. "Did you notice the first word on his sign?"

"You mean 'repent'?" The second man replied.

Bill took a sip of his coffee. "That's the word."

"So what?" interjected the first man.

Bill put his coffee cup down and looked at the two men sitting across from him.

"I've been thinking a lot lately about what it is that we do for a living---what it means to work for a hedge fund on Wall Street. We've made a ton of money. Our investors haven't been so fortunate. They've lost a lot of their money—some have lost everything."

The second man looked at the first, then back at Bill. "Welcome to the world of finance. You place your bets and take your chances. You know as well as me that derivatives are a complex and sophisticated financial instrument. Sometimes it can be hard..."

"Cut the bullshit," Bill interrupted. "No matter how you dress it up, it still boils down to the fact that we sold bad debt to good clients whose only mistake was to trust us."

"We did nothing illegal," the first man chimed in. "So what if we made a lot of money. The guys at the top made a lot more. We explained the terms and risks to our clients. We put it all in writing."

"Explained it my ass," Bill replied. He could feel his face turning red. "How can we explain something we don't even understand. Hell, Albert Einstein couldn't decipher the fine print in our client's contracts."

The second man shifted uncomfortably in his chair. "Bill, what's gotten into you? We all got record bonuses last year. It's not our fault that the investments went south. We followed the lead of the firm's senior partners. If anyone did, they were the ones that dropped the ball."

Bill drained the last of his coffee and placed his cup on the table. "I'll tell you what's gotten into me. For the most part, it's extinct on Wall Street—it's called a conscience. When I look at that old man's sign across the street, it's easy enough to believe that we have plenty to repent of."

The second man turned to Bill. "Speak for yourself, I'm just doing my job and supporting my family---all legal and above board."

"Maybe legal, but hardly above board," Bill replied with more than a hint of sarcasm.

Bill's companions slid their chairs back and stood up. "Come on Bill, we'll be late for work. It's Friday, you'll feel better after a long weekend."

As the two men crossed the street, they realized Bill had turned toward the old man with the sign.

"Pardon me, Mister."

The old man turned to the sound of Bill's voice.

"I'd like to know why you are standing here with that sign?"

"What's your name, son?"

"Bill."

"Well my name's Henry. Nice to meet you Bill."

"To answer your question, I'm fishing for souls."

"Fishing for souls? What kind of answer is that?"

"It's the only answer I've got. I'm fishing for souls and this here sign is my bait."

Bill rubbed his chin.

"So you don't really believe what your sign says is true?"

"Young friend, I don't believe it to be true, I *know* it to be true."

"How can you know something like that."

"I just do."

"Sounds like a crock to me."

The old man said nothing.

"The sign says repent."

"That's right."

"What am I supposed to repent of?"

"Whatever you need to repent of?"

"That's not much of an answer."

The old man pulled a toothpick out of his shirt pocket and placed in the corner of his mouth.

"I agree, it's not much of an answer, but it's enough.

"Enough for what?"

"Enough to get you moving to where you need to go."

"Well, Henry, my friends were wrong about you. You're not crazy, but I must say you don't make much sense."

"I'm not here to make sense."

Bill turned to leave, then stopped and looked into the old man's eyes.

"What's the point of repenting if the end is near—if it's all over anyway. What difference does it make?"

"Question is my young friend, what difference does it make to you?"

Bill looked at Henry then at a flock of pigeons swooping toward a high perch across the street. "I guess I'm not sure."

Henry pulled a pack of chewing gum from his shirt pocket and handed a stick to Bill. "Try a piece of 'Juicy Fruit'. It'll put a touch of sweet on the bad taste you're feeling inside you."

Bill popped the gum in his mouth.

Henry reached out and placed a hand on Bill's shoulder. "What's troubling you, son? What sorrow's got hold of you?"

Bill stared down at the sidewalk. "I got a big decision to make---maybe the biggest of my life."

He looked up. "I don't know why I'm telling you—I shouldn't."

Henry gently gave Bill's shoulder a gentle squeeze. "That's your call. Little choices along the path lead each of us to a place where a big decision is headed our way."

"I know," Bill replied, the strain clearly showing in his face. "I've made a lot of money with the firm I work for---some of it questionable. I mean, it's legal and all according to our corporate attorney, but our investors have gotten hurt—some even ruined---by the products we sold them."

Bill paused, pondering if he should say anything else.

Henry waved at a passerby and turned back to Bill."Legal don't necessarily make something right. Sometimes it does. Other times, legal covers a lot of darkness and hurt, makes folks feel better about something they should feel bad about."

Bill pulled out a handkerchief and blew his nose. "Yeah, it seems like what's left of my conscience has finally caught up with me. A fellow from the Justice Department wants me to testify against one of our senior partners. They aren't after me, or so they say, but apparently have something on him. They want me to help them---do the right thing. The right thing will cost me my job, an income my wife and daughter depend on. That's a hell of a price to pay."

"True enough," Henry replied. "That said, you don't seem too happy with the price you been paying."

"Paying for what?"

Henry flipped his toothpick into the trash can he was leaning on. "Sounds to me like you been paying a right heavy price for your self-respect. What price is that worth—or your soul for that matter? You reckon your family would rather have all of you or just the part you been showing them?"

Bill ran his hand through his hair. "Good question. Good question with a hard answer. That's what I noticed about your sign. If I repent and testify, the end is near. It will be over for me. We will have to make some hard changes—put a lot behind us—friends, standard of living and God knows what else."

Henry looked at Bill. "You know what you need to do and God knows what else. Like I said before, it's your call."

Bill offered his hand to Henry. "I thank you for your time. I've got an appointment to keep. My life's about to end as I've known it."

Bill turned to walk away.

"There's one more thing, Bill," Henry shouted.

"What's that?" Bill replied, looking back over his shoulder.

Henry's blue eyes danced and the corner of his mouth formed the hint of a smile. "The end is near, but so is the beginning."

ABOUT THE AUTHORS

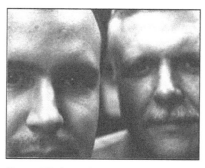

Scott Braswell works in creative media and communications. He has held positions in a number of professional and academic institutions, including The University of North Carolina, North Carolina State University and Hearst Media. His work includes writing feature stories, graphic design, video production and photography.

Michael Braswell is retired from East Tennessee State University where he taught criminal justice ethics. He has coauthored a Civil War novel, academic textbooks on ethics and other topics and two short story collections.